Zenas J. Gray

Prose and Poetry

of the Susquehanna and Juniata rivers

Zenas J. Gray

Prose and Poetry
of the Susquehanna and Juniata rivers

ISBN/EAN: 9783337238964

Printed in Europe, USA, Canada, Australia, Japan

Cover: Foto ©Andreas Hilbeck / pixelio.de

More available books at **www.hansebooks.com**

SUSQUEHANNA

AND

JUNIATA RIVERS.

EDITED BY

ZENAS J. GRAY,

1885.

HARRISBURG PUBLISHING CO.

HARRISBURG, PA.

TO MY FRIEND

WILLIAM MURRAY GRAYDON,

WHOSE LIFE AND WORK HAS BEEN IN CLOSE COM
MUNION AND SYMPATHETIC TOUCH WITH ALL
OF NATURE'S BEAUTIES OF MOUNTAIN,
FIELD AND RIVER—THIS

SIMPLE TRIBUTE
IS HUMBLY DEDICATED

BY

THE WRITER

June 12, 1842.

Prose and Poetry

Susquehanna and Juniata Rivers

WHY?

THERE is no reason why this book should not have been written years ago, nor is there a logical excuse for its appearance now. The public could have lived without it. It is believed, however, that the student of local history, the lover of our own beautiful rivers will, in time, learn to appreciate the labor of pen and pencil required in its compilation.

The Editor acknowledges many favors from the works of Dr. William H. Egle, numerous contributions from local writers and others who gave encouragement at every stage of the work. The illustrations are from photographs by I. Izmer, Eaton and Schriver, of Harrisburg, W. Bailey, of Columbia. A majority of the perfect illustrations were made from pictures especially painted by Edward B. Black, of Harrisburg, whose talent and genius shows in every line.

SUSQUEHANNA.

THROW broad thy gleaming waters bright,
  O Susquehanna! in thy flow,
  And let me lie and dream to-night
  Of days which once I seemed to know.
O river rolling from the dawn
  Of a new world and century,
Not yet, not yet, shall be thy song,—
  That in the future yet must be.

O broad blue river, in thy beams
  I see around me now the lands
Already growing dim like dreams
  In which are warring savage bands.
They come again as in a dream,
  Their shadows moving to and fro,
And watchfires on the hills that gleam
  In the red sunset's crimson glow.

Now like some gleaming sword all bright
  Unsheathed by some great God of old,
Thou severest with thy liquid light
  The darkness which is round thee rolled.
The turbid Tiber still doth flow
  By temples, aqueducts and domes,
It lot of dead days past doth know
  When heroes round it made their homes.

But thou, O river rolling on,
  It is the future which is thine;
A future when a brighter sun
  On brighter days shall proudly shine.
And in the distant years to come,
  Like fable, will it still be told
How a strange race, whose lips are dumb,
  Named thee in time far past and old.

  BENNETT BELLMAN.

UP STREAM.

 IP deep the broad paddles, send forward with swiftest stroke and agile leap the light canoe, cut the rough white caps with sharpened prow until naught but silvery gleams of churned spray mark the boat's pathway; spurn the noisome marshes of Spesutia island, and toward of the sand bars that hug, with treacherous embrace, the shadowy shore. Row carefully as you round Rocky Point, then bend to the oars for all danger is behind.

Dip! Dip! Dip! The oar locks creak, the craft bounds ahead; Carpenter's Point comes into full view, and the spires of Havre de Grace point into the horizon. A steamer passes with splashing wheels and hoarse whistle of recognition; to the left a topsail schooner rides gracefully on the crested waves, while sloops and smaller ships, with sails unfurled, drive onward toward the storm-washed Capes that guard the outlet to old ocean.

Deeper dip the oars as the breast of the current grows stronger and the waves line harder and more difficult to break. The shores come nearer and nearer, and the waters leap upon the beach to fall back into the waiting lap of the ebbing tide.

Dip! Dip! On and on! leaving behind the long, low marshes, the salt-laden waves and sand-crowned shores of historic Chesapeake Bay, where Neptune, forsaking his deepest kingdom, comes up in royal chariot to view the verdant hills of Maryland. Between the lusty oar strokes there comes the noise of town life, the busy, bustling monotone heard only in the sea-port cities; the wheezy puffing of tugs and steamers, the cheery call and song of sailor and longshoreman,—and the boat is in other waters.

Ah, the thrilling sensation! The boat has crossed the magic line and plows forward as if propelled by a mightier force; the waves have less resistance and the current exhibits a milder and gentler manner. There is a sparkling bewitchingness about the drops that roll from off the oar blades seen only in a tiny mountain stream, the babbling meadow brook and the big, cool spring that bubbles forth from beneath the spreading willow of some dear old home up, far up, among the Pennsylvania hills. The boat has indeed crossed the magic line; and the waters of the noble Susquehanna, with lingering echoes from Jack's Narrows, Iroquois, Wyalusing and Conewago, baptize the prow with silent blessings and invocations.

A SONG OF THE MARSHES.

I SING a song of the marshes,
    A melody seldom sung.
But the tune may find an answering note
    In the heart, though not from the tongue;
        'Tis a song of the tangled marshes,
            Of undergrowth, dank and tall,
        Shores kissed by laughing ripple
            And hugged by the waterfall.

A song of the gloomy marshes,
    Of swamp-land, malaria-bound,
Of weeds, pestilential and noisome,
    Where the snake and lizard are found;
        Where the river creeps in from its current
            And in glances loving and shy,
        Coquets with "pill-will-willet,"
            When he chances to wade by.

A song of reed-decked marshes,
    That none but the gunner knows,
Where game-birds live uncertain lives
    As the hunting season grows.
        These are the river marshes,
            And this the song I sing,
        Though the melody may lack sweetness
            To the theme I gladly cling.

SUSQUEHANNA AND JUNIATA RIVERS.

THE SONG.

Come to the marshes, bold hunters, come rowing,
   Daybreak is flushing the eastern sky;
The sun is just showing the horizon glowing
   And morning peeps forth from her aerie on high.
Make haste while the birds are guardedly sleeping,
   Row silently to the bush-grown isle,
Lest you startle the sentinels, faithfully keeping
   Their watch o'er the trusting ones, resting from toil.

Make haste with your boats, your guns hold ready—
   To the haunts of the canvas-back, mallard and teal
You are come. Row softly, and keep your arm steady,
   There's fun in the marshes, but death's on the trail.
Hush! dip your oars lightly, nature is list'ning,
   Steer not on the mud-fringed shallows too far,
Creep slowly beneath the bushes, all glist'ning
   With dew-drops wept by the morning star.

Hark, the rail bird, first to take warning!
   A thousand wings startle the mist-laden air,
The curlew, woodcock and plover dread morning,
   And swift from their lodgings they fly in despair.
Over there by that clump of brown-tasseled alders,
   Where the white-rooted valisneria grows,
Beyond the gray crowns of flood-washed bowlders,
   A sharp-eyed mallard his topknot shows

Aim sure, aye steady! Successful the slaughter,—
   Across the wide marshes few refugees fly,
The flock is depleted and blood-stained the water—
   Bag the game and for other victims we'll lie.
How joyous the sport! True hunters ne'er tire
   Of boat that is trusty and gun that is sure,
'Tis a pleasure exciting; all thoughts inspire
   Ambitions that know but river and moor.

ZENAS J. GRAY

FIRST EXPLORER.

CAPTAIN JOHN SMITH has the credit of being the discoverer and first explorer of the Susquehanna. When he returned to Jamestown with an elaborate account of what he had found and seen during his trip up the Chesapeake Bay, he little dreamed and knew, still less, the wealth and beauty of mountain, valley and river above, and far beyond the point where his boat stopped. Although a daring sailor and fearless fighter, Smith was distrustful of the Northern Indians, who in the eyes of the Englishmen, looked like giants. He feared treachery, notwithstanding at every landing he was met with evidences of friendship and hospitable welcome. This uncertain knowledge of the nature and intention of the natives kept Smith and his followers close to their barge which could sail only in the deeper waters. This was considered sufficient cause to prevent, or postpone further explorations though various reasons are given in addition to the contests for foothold in the new world that were being waged between rival kings for possession and maintenance of their royal prerogatives.

Mouth of the Susquehanna.

Captain Smith was, therefore, the recognized first white man to dip oars in the waters of the Susquehanna,—the glorious most beautiful and romantic river. This event occurred in 1608, the year after the settlement of Jamestown. Smith returned to England and in 1629 published a map of the Chesapeake Bay and its tributaries. It is a primitive and roughly executed drawing, but a truthful reflection of the limited knowledge of the art of draughting and the magnificent country it was designed to represent. According to his journal Smith sailed up the Susquehanna until the first rapids were reached.

before he learned the name of the river. At the falls a party of Indians met him, and from them he heard the word "Sasquesahanough," now called Susquehanna. The Indians whom Smith met at the falls, which some historians think was at, or near Conestoga creek, were of the Sasquesahanough, "people of the Falls River," who lived in fortified towns situated at points between the present sites of Harrisburg and Port Deposit.

As to the derivation of the word, Dr. William H. Egle says: "The first part, *Sasquesa*, meant Falls; the second part *Hanough*, is the Algonquin *hanne*, meaning *stream*. As applied to these people by their neighbors, it signifies very expressively '*The people of the Falls River*.' Through time the word was gradually changed to Sasquehannock, and finally to Susquehanna.'" Thus is very satisfactorily disposed of the claim of certain writers on Indian history that Susquehanna meant "The long crooked river."

Saude Island, near Port Deposit.

From the time of Smith's explorations until the coming of William Penn, few, if any, settlers dared to locate any distance from the Chesapeake Bay, the Delaware river and other navigable streams. These conditions were largely due to the warlike habits and revengeful attitudes of the tribes who looked upon the whites as robbers and usurpers, facts which were known to the Indians, having been exemplified in the New England Colonies. Then, too, the river not being navigable, ships from which protection might be sought and obtained could not pass the falls, communication with the upper country being possible with canoe and batteaux only. As a consequence foreign adventurers who came over in ships of deep draught placed little value on lands contiguous to a river not navigable.

It remained, however, for William Penn, the English Quaker, to bring into prominence a land of milk and honey, and to invite colonists and make possible their existence away from the Delaware, which seemed to be the magnet toward which the wealth, the brain, the bone and sinew of the adventurous and discontented Briton rushed with avaricious designs. Penn, as is well known, held, by virtue of his purchase, the river Susquehanna, all the islands therein and lands on both sides. He did not originate the plan of buying the Indians' lands but was an imitator of Calvert, who planted his Maryland colony in 1634; Roger Williams, the banished Quaker, who left Massachusetts for Rhode Island in 1636; the Swedes who bought land on the west shore of the Delaware in 1638, and Phillip Carteret, 1665, the then Governor of New Jersey. That he approved of the plan and held all such transactions as sacred and binding his whole life and doings in the New World is evidence.

Penn knew of the rich lands on the Susquehanna river and in 1684, two years after his

William Penn.

arrival here, and prior to his return to England, arranged with Governor Thomas Dongan of New York, to buy from the Five Nations "all the lands on the Susquehanna and that adjacent to the lakes in or near the province of Pennsylvania." Dongan succeeded well and gave to the colonists the first evidence of wholesale land-grabbing, of later years scantly termed syndicating, and which is commonly and cleverly practised.

William Penn was honest, but exacting and shrewd; he calculated the magnitude of the great deal and did not rest satisfied until the Dongan purchase was ratified and confirmed which took place September 13, 1700. The price paid for all this valuable territory was about five hundred dollars.

Following is a copy of the deed: "Sept. 13, 1700, Wistangh and Awiggey-Junkquagh, Kings or Sachems of the Susquehanna Indians, and of the river under that name and lands lying on both sides thereof. Deed to W. Penn for all the said river Susquehannough, and all the islands therein, and all the lands situate, lying and being on both sides of the said river, and next adjoining the same, to the utmost confines of the lands which are or formerly were, the right of the people or nation called the Susquehannough Indians, or by what name soever they were called, as fully and amply as we or any of our ancestors, have, could, might or ought to have had, hold or enjoyed, and also confirm the bargain and sale of the said lands, made unto Col. Thomas Dongan, now Earl of Limerick, and formerly Governor of New York whose deed of sale to Governor Penn we have seen.

This deed was still further confirmed the succeeding year by the Susquehanna, Potomac and Conestoga tribes who were dissatisfied and held aloof from the treaty of 1700.

The Susquehanna has its origin in a tiny lake or spring, less than a mile above Otsego Lake in New York, and flows southeast, receiving the rivers Unadilla and Chenango, then turning south enters Pennsylvania where it receives the Pittston Tioga, the West Branch and the

Source of the River, above Otsego Lake, N. Y.

Juniata, together with the numerous creeks that drain the valleys and empties itself into the Chesapeake Bay, at Havre de Grace, Maryland, 400 hundred miles from Lake Otsego, and 153 from its junction with the West Branch, at Northumberland. It is the longest river on the American continent not navigable, a condition made clear and comprehensible by the study and research of geologists.

The impression prevailed, and was shared by William Penn and his descendants relative and governmental, that the Susquehanna river was navigable, or that it could be made so by an insignificant outlay of money. The provincial government gave the matter some thought, but took no action, the colonial rulers following in the path trod by their predecessors. The settlers above the Conestoga were at a disadvantage as to means of transportation, the numerous rapids and dangerous currents being a standing menace to all plans suggested for their relief and benefit. It was not, therefore, until after the war of the revolution, when the population, which rapidly increased by the rush from foreign shores, sought wider and more promising fields for settlement, that public attention was more directly turned to the Susquehanna as a commercial highway. All schemes and suggestions put forward were discussed, ending in complete paralyzation by the reported and estimated magnitude of the undertaking, they knowing the immense expenditure of money that would be required to clear the channel for even light draught vessels. In the meantime, the ark, or flat boat was being poled from the Wyoming Valley to the Chesapeake, carrying the products of the backwoods settlements to be exchanged for domestic necessities and business traffic.

Francis Cummings, in 1807, made an extended tour along the Susquehanna, stopping at all villages enroute. He was interested in the transportation of products to the seaboard cities and observed closely the natural and existing conditions of the country through which he passed. A careful examination of the river from the tidewater to Harrisburg prompted him to note in his journal, viz.: "The Susquehanna would be one of the most useful rivers in the world—its different branches embracing a wonderful extent of country, settled or rapidly settling—were it not that it abounds with falls, shallows and rapids."

McColl's Ferry.

The completion of the canal around Conewago Falls, prior to 1800, which permitted of the passage of keel-bottom boats, had the effect of quieting agitation in the way of general river improvements. Finally, the Legislature, in 1825, became aroused and Samuel L. Wilson, Jabez Hyde and John McMeans, were named Commissioners to superintend the proposed improvements in the channel, between Northumberland and tidewater. From the records it will be seen that the work as prosecuted, because of the ridiculously small sum appropriated, was of no consequence, resulting in no advantage whatever. The Commissioners, in 1828, two years after their appointment, reported that $4,201.50 had been expended in improving the river from Columbia to Northumberland, and from Columbia to Tidewater $15,325.37.

Baltimore capitalists with more money than sagacity, in 1825, formed a company for the purpose of testing the practicability of operating steamboats between York Haven and Sun-

ferry. The entire stock was immediately taken, three boats were built, viz: the "Codorus," "Pioneer," and "Susquehanna," all of which made their trial trips in the fall of the year. Behind all this so-called progressive event was a scheme so frequently and successfully conducted in the intervening years 1825–1840,—that of robbing and plundering the State by genteel methods for decency's sake called appropriations. The Baltimore steamboat company was not alone in their prospective plans, but were backed and encouraged by native Pennsylvanians. Although it was intended to impress the State Legislature with the allurements and consequent rich returns from the establishing of a system of steamboats, the enterprising conspiracy failed of its object. The steamboats, loaded with enthusiastic passengers, steamed up to the improvised wharf at Mulberry street, Harrisburg, where the legislators stood waiting to be impressed. But no appropriation was forthcoming and the hopes of the projectors were not realized. The result is easily summed up. The "Pioneer" was not provided with sufficient power to stem the currents of the various rapids and was frequently grounded. In April, 1826, the "Codorus" ran into a sand-bar at Montgomery's Ferry, where it lay for a week. This boat made a trip up the Susquehanna to a line separating Pennsylvania from New York, and is believed to be the first boat propelled by steam ever placed on American waters. About the same time the "Susquehanna," when near Berwick, exploded its boiler. Of the passengers, two were killed and a number wounded, Representative Probst of Columbia county, being among the injured. The boat was a total wreck. In 1834 the citizens of Harrisburg attempted to secure national legislation for the purpose of "opening a steamboat and sloop communication between the Chesapeake Bay and the lakes, by way of the Susquehanna river." Congress then, and later on, refused to make an appropriation, which created the suspicion that the Government at Washington was in sympathy with the management of the canals along the Susquehanna, which were under construction by the State. When it is recalled that this noble old river drains nearly fourteen millions of acres of land, still in the infancy of enterprise and production at the time referred to, there was intelligent reason in the prophecy made in 1841, "that in a few years more the present canal system will be inadequate to carry off the products of the Susquehanna Valley." The honorable citizen and patriot had sincere and unbounded confidence in the future greatness of the old Keystone State. It was with this same confidence and individual zeal that again lead to a movement looking to the navigation of the Susquehanna, largely brought about by the reckless and extravagant expenditures of public money in the construction of canals by the infamous Canal Board. It was proposed to again attempt the removal of rocks in the main channel; to construct locks of sufficient capacity to allow the passage of heavy draught steamboats, and build canals, though at considerable distance from the river, that the greater falls and rapids might be overcome. Visionary as this way now seems, it will be remembered that millions of dollars were being spent annually on the canals and railroads had not yet come into use; the advantage of the desired improvements being apparently far beyond the ken of the most enthusiastic believer. But the advocates of navigation persisted, contesting every foot of legislative ground, finally succumbing but without striking their flag. The obnoxious Canal Board held the purse strings of the Commonwealth within its grasp, controlled elections, made the Executive a mere figurehead and brought the credit of the State to the door of bankruptcy. There were millions for canals, but nothing for river improvements. And thus ended all efforts in favor of making navigable the Susquehanna river.

WHEN THE BASS BITE BEST.

HEN the North is breezy and cool and clear,
 Lifting the low blue hills in sight,
When the waters are dimpled beyond the pier
And clouds sail idly over the mere—
  Oh, that is the time for the bass to bite.

When boughs grow bare and apples fall
 With every flaw from the windy West,
When the frost is white on the orchard wall
And the river is blue at the passing squall—
  Oh, that is the time when the bass bite best.

When paths are blind with a drift of leaves
 And nuts lie thick in the yellow grass,
When barns are bursting with garnered sheaves
"Ripenirt berries"—full to the eaves—
  Oh, that is the time for the wary bass.

With a silvery shiner far below
 Tugging away at a silken thread
In a cove where the quiet currents flow
And purple shadows come and go
  And a bit of blue sky overhead.

Too soon the western hills grow black
 With lone pine looming above their crest
In silhouette—too soon, alack!
Do far lights glimmer to guide us back—
  For that is the time when the bass bite best.

SAFE HARBOR OR CONESTOGA.

AFE HARBOR is built on or near the site of the old Indian town Conestoga, which figured so conspicuously in the early settlement of the Susquehanna Valley. The village was located on the banks of the stream which took its name from the tribe living thereon, and was known to the first white man who paddled up the "River of the Great Falls," being the principal meeting place or Council town of the tribes that paid tribute to the Iroquois, or Six Nations. To it came annually representatives from the Southern and Western Indians to confer together concerning the encroachment of the whites, who while in actual possession of the best lands on the New England coast, the Delaware river, and Chesapeake Bay showed avaricious desires and partiality for the still richer lands lying contiguous to the Susquehanna. How well they succeeded in their designs the student of history knows, and the descendants of the early settlers and landholders can tell. The land skirting the Conestoga creek is the most fertile in the State, rich in products, native and cultivated. The Tuckey Hills that form the east bank of the river and shore gradually to the north, rise up in great bluffs giving to the scenery an aspect of charming wildness and sublimity.

To the Conestoga in 1701 came William Penn, the proprietor of the country, who met with a warm welcome at the hands of the Indians because of their confidence in him and his intentions to deal honestly with them. In 1705 James Logan, representing the proprietor, spent some time making inquiries concerning certain traders who had built cabins in the neighborhood. Governor Evans, with a retinue of petty officers, visited Conestoga in 1707; likewise Governor Gookin in 1710, and Governor Keith in 1721, the latter to investigate charges against two traders, John and Edward Cartlidge, then in jail for various alleged misdemeanors, the principal being that of reducing the Indians to break faith with the English and favor the French.

Safe Harbor.

On this spot the Paxtang Boys meted out tardy justice to a degenerate remnant of treacherous and calumnious savages, forever putting a quietus on the atrocious murders committed almost daily in the villages north of the Conestoga creek. This act of extermination occurred on the night of December 14th, 1763. The Paxtang Boys were frontiersmen of the ideal type, could penetrate the bull's eye with a rifle ball, and lift the scalp from the head of an Indian with neatness and dispatch. All were prominent in the affairs of life and early resorted to measures as a last remedy for the desperate condition of the frontier, brought about by the difference as to the treatment of suspected Indians and the policy outlined by the proprietors and Quakers as against the judgment and demands of the landholders and frontiersmen. The few Indians that escaped the slaughter at Conestoga, being absent from the village the night of the attack, were on the morning of December 27th, killed in the Lancaster workhouse, whither they had fled after the bloody affair at Conestoga, the Rangers overpowering the keeper and defying the authorities. Notwithstanding the presence of a company of militia in the town, the Paxtang Boys had their own way and went to their homes confident of the greater safety from the scalping knife, conditions that followed immediately thereafter.

With the disappearance of the Indians from the Conestoga there came settlers who increased in numbers and prospered. The valuable mines of ore were early developed, a furnace and rolling mill built and bars manufactured. The rails for the first complete equipment of the Pennsylvania railroad were made here. The Conestoga creek was at an early date, rendered navigable for large boats by the erection of a series of dams and locks, a still larger dam being constructed across the Susquehanna about 300 yards below the mouth of the creek. Boats were then towed across the river by a steamboat to the Tidewater canal. But a great change has come over this community. Business has fallen off, the canal is abandoned, with here and there the remains of an old lock to tell where the boatman's horn once waked the echoes among Lancaster's green hills. As to the dam across the river there is but a faint trace of it left, the floods of thirty years ago completely demolishing it. Near the site of the old dam is "Indian Rock," a massive bowlder containing hieroglyphics, signs and characters indicative of their aboriginal history. This rock is well preserved and quite easy of access during the summer months. Safe Harbor is a sleepy old village, one-half of its houses being in ruins while the other half is apparently affected by the same

Scene near Safe Harbor.

destroying influences. The existence of three licensed taverns may account, to a considerable degree, for the desolate appearance that is everywhere visible. The place was in great repute for its prolific fishing grounds, but since the destruction of the dam the visits of the fishermen grow less year by year.

Experiments for steam navigation were first made in the Conestoga, as early as 1760, by one William Henry, who partially succeeded, but his boat accidently sunk and he died soon thereafter. Near the historic stream was born Robert Fulton, who successfully used the steam engine for the propelling of boats. Fulton went to Europe, where he studied painting under Benjamin West, but returning to America, he resolved to navigate rivers by means other than sail and oar. This was in 1806. Two years later he built the boat "Clermont" with which he steamed up the Hudson to Albany and returned. Fulton died in 1815, after years of toil, attended by successes and disappointments.

A DAM NUISANCE.

WHEN April comes on the shadfly's wing
'Tis a sign that shad are ripe, and Spring
The luscious creature has bared her arms
To show the world voluptuous charms
That passing crowds look up to see
And love her for her modesty.
She hears the fisherman's tale of woe
From Havre de Grace to Otsego,
How he raves from morn to night,
His moral tone is in a plight.
He seeks for aid, he knows not where,
His life has many loads to bear,
For the savory shad is seen no more
Above Columbia's smoke-wrapt shore.

The sound of wrath comes floating down
From Nanticoke to Sunbury town,
Past the Notch where Girty's cave
Looks out on Susquehanna's wave.
Still on and on, till isle and shore
Clasp hands at Conewago's roar,
Till Falmouth hears—alas the psalm!—
"O dam Columbia! Columbia dam!
O doleful nuisance! Not a sham
Is this dam Columbia! Columbia dam!"
The waves have washed, the waves have worn
Its broad old breast the floods have torn
Yet laughs at storms—so stout, I'm sure
A thousand years it will endure
Through centuries we'll sing the psalm—
"O dam Columbia! Columbia dam!"

COLUMBIA AND WRIGHTSVILLE.

COLUMBIA and Wrightsville, the twin cities on the Susquehanna, are united by a mammoth wooden bridge 5620 feet long. The first bridge was built in 1814, the same year that Columbia was incorporated as a borough. It was partly destroyed by the ice-flood of 1832. In the latter part of June, 1863, it was burned, to prevent Lee's army, that was imbued with such fatal results at Gettysburg, from getting a foothold east of the Susquehanna. The entire structure was immediately rebuilt.

For many years Columbia, so delightfully situated on the banks of the river, was the terminus of the Philadelphia and Columbia railroad, where it connected with the canal already built and in operation along the upper Susquehanna. The advantages of these improvements brought the town into prominence and its business

Columbia from the Hill.

prospered rapidly and grew in wealth and importance. All freight was transshipped here, and together with its iron and lumber industries the place assumed airs that, compared with to-day, the imagination is unequal to the task. All the vast lumber interests of the mountain regions beyond the Kittatinny range centered here where saw-mills converted the crude lumber into building material, that found its way into every community. When rafting was at its prodigious height, Columbia was at the zenith of its prosperous career. The decline was gradual until after the rebellion when the raftsman disappeared and his well remembered figure, rowdyish and attire has but a niche in crowded memories.

Scores of men now prominent in financial and business circles here laid the foundation of fortunes and world-wide prominence, and from the old borough have gone out into the world men as good, grand and noble as ever basked in the sunshine of a dazzling future.

The first settler was Robert Barber, a native of Yorkshire, England, who purchased one thousand acres of land from the Penns. This tract extended to the river and included the present site of Columbia. Barber came to Lancaster county from Chester about 1726. He induced others to emigrate with him, among whom was John Wright, after whom Wrightsville was named. Shortly after Barber's arrival at the Susquehanna, efforts were put forth to make Columbia the county seat. Barber had himself elected sheriff, building a log jail to forestall any subsequent movement that might be made favoring some other locality which however failed of its purpose. In Barber's log jail was confined James Annesley, who was the rightful Lord Altham and grandson of the celebrated Duke of Buckingham. The mother of James died in 1822, the lad being in his seventh year. His father had formed an liaison with a Miss Gregory, who schemed to marry the elder Altham and desired the removal of the child. To accomplish her object she poisoned the mind of the Lord against his son by telling him that James was not his lawful child. He was placed in a school in Dublin by his father, who died suddenly soon after. Richard, uncle of James was an accomplished villain and determined to possess the estate by getting rid of both his nephew James and the Gregory woman. In the person of the latter Richard found a foe worthy of the steal he proposed perpetrating, being compelled to pay her a large sum of money that enabled her to escape to the continent where she disappeared. In April,

Columbia Tunnel.

1728, James was kidnapped and carried to Philadelphia, where he was sold as a redemptioner to a German farmer. In a few months he ran away and being caught was confined in Sheriff Barber's log jail. He possessed a wonderfully sweet voice, with which he frequently entertained the ladies of the village, rendering the choicest Irish and Scotch selections. After being released from jail, which was about 1740, he worked for a farmer living on the Lancaster turnpike. One day he met two Irishmen from near Dublin, who recognized the young lord, and who later on returned with him to Ireland, and testified at the trial of the unscrupulous uncle. James died shortly after securing his rights and valuable estates, and his uncle was again in undisputed possession.

The old ferry between Columbia and Wrightsville was operated for many years by the Wrights, the course being about midway between the dam and the bridge. It was a simple affair but served the day and purpose for which it was designed. Along about the year 1745 James Wright built the little stone mill on Shawnee Run, where flour was made for the soldiers belonging to Braddock's expedition. The manufacture of iron and iron products is still carried on extensively, the advantages and resources of the place being equal to any in the State.

The Twin Cities are known for their enviable positions in the shad fishing industry, the early construction of the famous dam giving them a well-enjoyed monopoly in that direction. The first shad said to have been caught here with a seine was after 1760. During the fishing season, commencing about April 1st, and continuing into the month of May, the broad stretch of river below the dam fairly swarms with fishermen, who toil all night long with varied success. Of late years Columbia has lost its old-time prestige for shad fishing, the pirates farther down being accused of using gill nets and other illegal devices for catching fish.

It is related by historians that Wrightsville narrowly escaped being made the Capital of the United States. General Washington, who frequently crossed at Wright's Ferry, impressed with the natural beauty of the location, picturesque surroundings and security from foes, strongly urged upon Congress the advantages to be gained. Other prominent men advocated the town on the Susquehanna, but a small majority prevailed against and in favor of the present city on the Potomac.

The Tidewater canal, extending from Columbia to Havre de Grace, a distance of 45 miles, was chartered by the States of Pennsylvania and Maryland, in 1835, with a paid up capital of $1,500,000. It was originally intended to construct the canal on the east side of the Susquehanna. But in 1836 the route was changed to the west side of the river. On account of the unforeseen difficulties the cost of construction exceeded the estimate of the chief engineer, Edward F. Gay, the total cost being about $4,000,000. The work was pushed vigorously forward, and late in the fall of 1839, water was first admitted that the banks might be thoroughly tested. The event was celebrated with pomp and ceremony and a free excursion from Columbia to Havre de Grace, in which many distinguished citizens of both States participated. It was then that Hon. Nicholas Biddle, of Philadelphia, made his famous speech on internal improvements. It is told that a number of the excursionists had not yet returned home when the banks gave way in many places washing tons of earth from where it had just been laid, creating damages and disaster that was most disheartening. But the crevasses were repaired and the canal opened to the public use the following Spring. The greatest amount of revenue from boat tolls received in any one year was $225,000, collected in 1865.

Ever since its erection the Columbia dam has borne the execrations and denunciations of upper-river residents, sportsmen in particular, who blame the scarcity of the shad to the existence of this artificial obstruction. Laws innumerable and legislation without limit have failed to effect its removal or even modification. Fishways have been placed in the dam at great cost to the State, in addition to appropriations for other improvements that have proven worthless. Storms have swept over the old dam, floods have torn away a portion of its mighty bulwark, and spring freshets have taken a turn at demolition, but the handiwork of a former generation remains to vex the angler of to-day. A long list of floods, viz: 1817, 1846, 1857, 1865, 1868, 1875, and 1889 left the structure wrecked and broken, but the damages were as quickly repaired. The dam, together with the Tidewater canal, were, in 1872, leased by the Philadelphia and Reading Railroad Company, who have since operated them.

The Tidewater Canal, so far as concerns general uses for transportation, local or otherwise, is practically abandoned, scarcely more than a score of boats passing through the Wrightsville lock during 1892. With these conditions, and existing facts for argument, why not remove the Columbia dam, that upriver fishermen and lovers of planked shad may revel in the delights of taking and partaking of them without loss of temper or begrudged collapse of the domestic treasury?

Passing up-stream one sees the continual smoke of furnace and hears the roar of trains thundering along bearing their freight to the uttermost parts of the world. The beholder is awed by the grandeur and picturesqueness of the variety of landscape spread before him. Emerging from the mountainous formation is a jagged ridge, its abrupt cliffs dipping directly into the water. Through it is the "Columbia Tunnel," alike familiar to all travelers of the railroad and boatman. Chiques Rock, the highest and boldest headland south of the Shikalamy bluffs, overlooks the river for miles limited only by the Conewago hills on the north and the Turkey hills southward. Chiques creek empties here, a name reverenced wherever a son of Lancaster roams or has a fixed habitation. The rich and seemingly inexhaustible deposit of iron ore in the vicinity affords every facility for the manufacture of iron. Numerous furnaces are here, their products being the principal basis upon which rests the solidity and substantial prosperity of the surrounding country. At the foot of the celebrated rock is the old Haldeman mansion, a stately land-mark that speaks of sixty years of progress and

Chiques Rock.

improvement. It was built by the late Professor Haldeman, an eminent scholar and mineralogist and is a type of ancestral archi-tecture standing alone by "the beautiful rolling river."

Marietta is a pretty town, delightfully situated on the river shore, along which it extends for nearly two miles. It was founded as a rival to Columbia, an act having been passed in 1811 au-thorizing the erection of a bridge across the Susquehanna, but the friends of the Columbia project secured an appropriation from the State and the bridge was built there. The place was originally known as Anderson's ferry. An-derson was one of the pioneers and made every preparation to conduct his ferry on a business

Marietta, from Old Accomac Tavern.

basis. He cut a road through the York hills that lead travel down to old Accomac tavern and offered special inducements to patrons. But the Columbia bridge ruined him finan-cially and the ferry suffered a decline. The Accomac tavern is still a favorite resort for fishing parties from Lancaster and York. A few miles north of Marietta is Donegal Presbyterian church, it being the parent church of the Scotch-Irish settlements on the Susquehanna, and from which sprang all the many congregations in Central and Southern Pennsylvania. The first church at Donegal was built prior to 1700.

Wild Cat Glen is the most gorgeous piece of romantic scenery along the entire river. It is on the York county shore, one and a half miles above Marietta. A deep, narrow canon piercing the high hills, with rock-piled walls and precipitous ledges, with trees of every variety of growth crowning the topmost ridges and dark ravines. Narrow pathways lead into the deepest recesses of the glen, along the noisy stream of pure water that tumbles and dashes in rollicking, reckless humor down the weird chasm, forming cascades and miniature falls that again spread out into tiny lakes and pools to again disappear in its tortuous descent to the river below. The glen was once quite popular, visitors from all parts of the country being attracted thereto. There is always blowing through the gorge breezes delightful and refreshing, and weary humanity may find rest and fascination in the wild scenes surrounding. The conveniences for a trip through the glen are admirable, paths leading in all directions and easy stairways and bridges spanning the deeper and more dangerous chasms. At the entrance to the glen, a few yards back from the shore, stands a large, roomy building with all conveniences for picnic parties or those who desire to spend a longer period. The facilities for boating and fishing are first-class; the locality being favorable in every respect. The place was once secured for the purpose of making it a permanent resort for members of the Masonic order, but the project failed of its realization.

Other towns of old-time prominence in the days of boating and rafting are Bainbridge and Collins station. The

Wild Cat Glen Falls, and View from Road.

former was once the site of the Indian town named Dekanoagah, the village of the Conoy or Ganawese tribe, commonly called "Flat-heads." A large collection of skulls, arrows, points, axes, beads, pottery, etc., was made from excavations for the canal. Below the town John Haldeman built a grist-mill and hauled the flour to Chester, where it found a market.

THE BOATMAN'S CALL.

AWAKE, awake, Lock-keeper! Let the boat drop through,
  We're drivin' hard to reach the lower bay;
Autumn's fadin' mighty rapid, winter's comin' too,
  Then the horn will cease its callin' night and day.
Open wide the drippin' gates, fill up the shiny lock,
  The water is impatient to rush on;
Hear the bugle notes a-tootin'! Far away! then wander back
  Like the memory of friendships lost and gone.
      O hear the horn! "Toot-a-too, too, too!"
        Make ready, we are comin'! Driver, slow-ow-o!
      'Toot-a-too, too, too! Toot-a-too, too, too-oo!'
        Away we onward go.

By fair romantic valleys, where Juniata's tide
  And Susquehanna's waters float along,
Through echoin' mountain passes—Old Kittatinny's pride—
  I've sat on deck and sang the joyous song.
The boatman's life has charms, the recollections plain,
  I like to go a-dreamin' of the past;
Though my forehead is wrinkled, my heart is young again,
  And I know the sentiment will always last.
      Hear the bugle blow! "Toot-a-too, too, too!"
        Make ready for our comin'! Driver, slow-ow-o!
      'Toot-a-too, too, too! Toot-a-too, too, too-oo!'
        Gladly we onward go.

I've been snubbin' long the towpath nearly fifty years,
  I've seen my share, had tears and frolics, too;
The steam cars have outdone us, we're crowded to the rear,
  The boatman's shadows grow more dim and few.
The packet is no longer seen—its rate of speed too slow
  To suit this age of rush and enterprise;
Soon the Locks will be deserted,—the grizzled captains go
  On the final trip beyond the nightless skies.
      O hear the horn! "Toot-a-too, too, too!"
        Steady there, steady! Driver, slow-ow-o!
      'Toot-a-too, too, too! Toot-a-too, too, too-oo!'
        Hopefully we onward go.

                                    ZENAS J. GRAY.

FALLS OF CONEWAGO.

A SHORT distance below the junction of the Conewago creek with the Susquehanna, at the extremity of Elliot's, now Duffy's Island, are the great falls of Conewago, the most dangerous rapids in the long list of obstructions to inland navigation. The Conewago Hills look down upon either shore and the natural scenery is of the wildest and most picturesque character. A great ledge of rocks stretches across the entire width of the river, irregular, massive and formidable in withstanding the rush and the fury of the centuries of floods. On the York county side the falls rise to a height of eighteen feet, terminating in scattered boulders of trap rock at Falmouth, on the east shore.

In 1793 the Conewago Canal Company was organized, the object being to facilitate the passage of flat boats and improve navigation in general. Through the efforts of this company the first canal on the Susquehanna was constructed. It was about one mile

Conewago Falls.

long, extending from the head of the rapids to where the York Haven mills now stand. It proved a paying investment, there being no railroads or artificial waterways, even the Conestoga wagon was unknown and the transportation of merchandise and all other kinds of commodities depended solely upon the ark or river boat. York Haven grew into a thriving and prosperous village, large stone warehouses were built by Baltimore capitalists, who made extensive preparations for sustaining a wheat market. Before this canal was completed, about 1794, a German miller, Jacob Kreider, residing on the Juniata at Huntingdon, ran the Conewago rapids with an ark loaded with flour and produce, successfully carrying it to Baltimore. For upwards of thirty years the boatman was king of the river and the most prominent and useful character in the prosperous and growing country beyond the Kittatinny range. However, with the construction of the canal from Harrisburg to Columbia and the Tidewater canal below, by which a through route to the

Chesapeake Bay was secured, the glory of York Haven passed away. The big warehouses fell into ruins and the river traffic of seventy years ago is a matter of history. Another canal for the carrying of boats around the falls was constructed on the east shore of the river, from Falmouth to Bainbridge, traces of which may yet be seen.

In the days when shad fishing above Columbia was a profitable industry, Conewago Falls figured conspicuously in profitable returns and was also a popular resort for anglers who wielded the rod for pleasure and entertainment. A number of fisheries located above the falls did an extensive business supplying the farmers on both sides of the river with choice shad. At the Conewago fisheries the men employed would rest during the day until about six p. m., when the seine was used to make a haul, followed by a rest until midnight, when they would start in again and fish until sunrise. During the spring season shad and salmon were so plenty that at certain places in the open current the shoals could be seen distinctly from the rocky shore and fish of enormous lengths would swim along, careless of the lookers on. But all this is changed. The erection at intervals along the river, of dams to promote slack water navigation has destroyed this once popular industry, until only the fisherman's legend or worn tale is inherited by succeeding generations.

Bass fishing at the falls is still indulged in and large strings of the favorite fish are caught annually. The innumerable rocks on the upper and lower ripples is an excellent hiding place for the bass which play at hide-and-seek with tantizing effect upon the seeker. Its gameyomeness, wonderful strength, plucky qualities and great table merits places the bass on the first course, unrivaled and undisputed. Fishing at Conewago is attended with considerable risk and manual caution is required to keep the boat from swinging into the dangerous and swift-running current.

CONEWAGO

CONEWAGO! Conewago! Pride of forest,
    Home of Nature's first adored,
How thy praises breathed and chanted
    To the topmost peaks have soared.
Up and down the broad old river
    Far away among the hills,—
Conewago! Conewago! How thy fondest
    Memory thrills.

O the rugged, wildest beauty of the
    Spray-bathed rock and isle;
O the dashing, splashing, crashing as
    The waters cast a smile.
Then with rumble, grumble, tumble
    And a playing hide-and-seek,
Drop to rest in calmer current from
    The mighty struggle weak.

Conewago! Conewago! Rich in legend
    And in fame,
Bravest pioneers have left thee
    Something other than a name,—
Penn and Haldeman and Kreider,
    Barber, Anderson and Wright,—
Proudest heroes of the century,
    Born to conquer, pray or fight.

Conewago! Conewago! Beautiful
    And grand thy place'—
When the early mists have lifted
    Like a veil from off thy face,
When the summers that would kiss thee
    Come with sunshine and cheer,
Conewago! Conewago! Ah, thy name
    And fame art dear.

ZENAS J. GRAY

THE RED HOUSE.

BOVE the Conewago Falls, and almost touching the rapids, is Elliott's island, while further up, probably a half-mile, opposite Goldsboro, and lying toward the York county shore, is another large body of land known as Shelly's island. They are the largest islands in the Susquehanna, and are noted for their productiveness and value as farm lands, being peculiarly adapted to the cultivation of tobacco, although other crops are grown with like prodixity. The area of Elliott's island is about four hundred acres and Shelly's two hundred and sixty acres. At one time they were considered the choicest fishing rights on the river.

Shelly's island is the more popular among sportsmen, it being located in the midst of the finest fishing and ducking grounds to be found between Havre de Grace and Otsego Lake. It is the home of the Red House Fishing and Gunning Club, composed of a score of ardent watermen whose fixed habitation is Harrisburg. Of late years the Capital City has become famous for the large number of enthusiasts who dwell within its gates, but who at uncertain and frequent intervals steal away from business and professional cares and seek the delightful shade of mountain, the cool, invigorating breezes of charming river scenes, or the quiet, restful life of the cosy and cheerful farmhouse. It is this sensible—and growing more general—desire to bid a temporary farewell to fret and worry that continues to encourage outdoor life and relaxation found only beyond the city's boundary. A most delightful spot where one may commune with Nature, where a day's outing may be enjoyed to the fullest extent and gratification is at the cheery old Red House.

Far removed from the ordinary haunts of men where the echoes of the street cannot penetrate, where there's naught but brightest sunshine, purest and health-giving air, and where peace and pleasure exclusively reign, what wonder that life passes as one glorious, voluptuous dream, and legends of Arca-

Red House, Looking Toward the Falls.

dian bliss become a reality. The club house is situated on the southern point of the island, near the west shore, and at an elevation of eighteen feet above low water mark. The building is one of the oldest on the Susquehanna, having been erected in 1787. It is built of logs, chinked and daubed and weatherboarded. It is one and a half stories high, with steep roof sloping down over a broad, open porch, facing the South, thus affording a magnificent and fascinating panorama of river, here and there studded with smaller islands, and the long range of Conewago hills in the perspective. Sitting on the old-fashioned porch, one is within sight and sound of the mighty rapids, and the weird noise of the waters call to mind the important part the old house has played in the drama of civilization and progress that crept up the Susquehanna, battling against the savage cruelty of the Indian, the treachery of French and English, and the deceit of the so-called peace-loving Quaker. Those were stirring times, and the Red House was one of the silent actors surviving all others. It is a precious relic of the past, and its century of years but makes it more hallowed to those who have partaken of the modern hospitality so liberally dispensed beneath its moss-grown roof. For many years it was used as a tavern and patronized solely by sailors on the old flat boats and their successors, the raftsmen, from the up-river lumber regions. Its color has been red since the time it was first occupied and was distinguished thus from the "White House" at Highspire. Successive generations have given proof of their fidelity to old customs by renewing its carmine hue on stated occasions. The interior is supplied with necessary comforts and its walls decorated with numerous exhibits of the taxidermist's art and trophies of the rod and gun. The Red House is a half-hour's row from Goldsboro station, on the Northern Central railroad.

THE SONG MY PADDLE SINGS.

Saw Mill at Goldsboro.

West wind, blow from your prairie nest,
Blow from the mountains, blow from the west,
The sail is idle, the sailor too;
O, wind of the west we wait for you.
Blow, blow!
I have wooed you so,
But never a favor you bestow.
You rock your cradle the hills between,
But scorn to notice my white lateen.

I stow the sail and unship the mast:
I wooed you long but my wooing's past;
My paddle will lull you into rest.
O drowsy wind of the drowsy west,
Sleep, sleep,
By your mountain steep,
Or down where the prairie grasses sweep.
Now fold in slumber your laggard wings,
For soft is the song my paddle sings.

August is laughing across the sky,
Laughing while paddle, canoe and I
Drift, drift
Where the shores uplift
On either side of the current swift

The river rolls in its rocky bed,
My paddle is plying its way ahead.
Dip, dip,
While the waters flip
In foam as over their breast we slip.

And, oh, the river runs swifter now
The eddies circle about my bow
Swirl, swirl!
How the ripples curl
In many a dangerous pool awhirl!

And far before me the rapids roar
Fretting their margins forevermore
Dash, dash,
With a mighty crash
They seethe and tumble and bound and splash.

Be strong, O paddle! be brave canoe!
The reckless waves you must bear me through
Reel, reel,
On your trembling keel,
But never a fear my craft will feel.

We've raced the rapid, we're far ahead,
The river slips through its silent bed.
Sway, sway,
As the bubbles spray
And fall in tinkling tunes away

And up the hills against the sky,
A fir tree rocking its lullaby.
Swings, swings,
Its emerald wings,
Swelling the song that my paddle sings.

                                    E. P. JOHNSON

MIDDLETOWN AND STEELTON.

MIDDLETOWN, situated at the mouth of the Swatara creek, was called by the Indians who had a village there "Swahadowry." The name Middletown was given it because of it being midway between Carlisle and Lancaster. It is a delightful place of residence, and its business and financial interests are creditably represented. It was laid out in 1755, by George Fisher, who inherited the land from his father, a Philadelphia merchant. It soon grew into prominence as a harbor for river boats and place of exchange. In 1779, during one of the Indian wars, the small boats, or batteaux used by General Sullivan's army were built here. Until the year 1794, when John Kreider first ran the Conewago Falls, Middletown, sometimes called Portsmouth, was considered the head of navigation, but after that period rafts and arks were piloted through to Baltimore with safety and greater profits. The town has suffered many fluctuations of fortune, due largely to the public improvements made by the State, and which directly concerned its prosperity by reason of its location at the junction of the Union and Pennsylvania canals, and the building of the railroad by way of Mount Joy, abandoning to a great extent, the re-shipping of freight to Columbia by the river route. The Union canal, long since abandoned, was projected in 1762 and completed in 1827, and was the first of all public improvements. William Penn is said to have visited the Swatara village in 1701, intending to proceed on up the Susquehanna, but was prevented by the prevalence of some disease supposed to be small-pox, then epidemic at certain points. Francis Cumming, in 1807, stopped over night in Middletown, at the General Washington Inn, kept by the widow Wentz. He was evidently delighted with the treatment received and the landlady as well. He describes the view down the river, from the porch of the inn, as very fine and the river as a noble stream. He tells of the plentifulness of rock fish, perch, mullet, eels, suckers, catfish, and white salmon, but says: "the inhabitants are too lazy to do anything except that which will give them money, and that is used to procure whiskey." The first steel made in America was produced here in 1795, from the furnace of Daniel and Thomas Stubbs. The completion of the Harrisburg, Portsmouth and Mount Joy railroad in 1836 was an event celebrated here with considerable pomp and enthusiasm, a "special train" with cars containing eighteen persons each, being run from Harrisburg.

One of the oldest churches in the country is still standing, though not used for congregational purposes. Old St. Peter's Lutheran church was built in 1767, and stands in the midst of the old graveyard, where repose the ashes of the early settlers. The interior is in a fair state of preservation.

Opposite Middletown, in the center of the river, is Hill Island, a large tract of land surrounded by water at all seasons of the year. The lower part of the island is cultivated, but the upper part terminates in a high bluff with a steep descent of two hundred feet to the river below. The top is covered with trees and immense rock, through which it is difficult to pass. Here, in 1844, the religious sect called Millerites made preparation to

Hill Island.

ascend heavenward in accordance with the prophecy of their leader, Miller, who predicted the Millennium. It was a cold day in the month of December when the little band crossed over to the island from which they were to bid farewell to every earthly tie. They were attired in white robes made expressly for the occasion, all other worldly possessions being left behind. All day long they sang and prayed and waited for the angel to pilot them into the land beyond, but night came down and still no sign of the Millennium. One of the brethren, a sort of doubting Thomas and possessed of little enthusiasm or confidence in the result, was overcome with fatigue and fell asleep. In the meantime a drizzling rain set in, and to keep warm huge bonfires were lighted, which shed a brilliant ray all about the assembly. The careless and sleeping brother awoke with a sudden start. Looking around with an expression of mingled resignation and surprise, he drolly remarked: "Well, in hell just as I expected."

The ascension was a failure; and the participants in after years told of their experience as one would relate a joke.

On the shore of the river, midway between Middletown and Highspire, is the "White House," a large three-story frame structure facing the open river, with a lawn shaded by thrifty trees and reaching to the pebbly shore. It is a relic of rafting days and known to every raftsman that ran the Susquehanna. It is one of the few old taverns built for the

The White House.

exclusive accommodation of rivermen. Here the lumbermen disposed of their rafts to dealers from Middletown, Goldsboro and York, or arranged to float their lumber on to Baltimore. The pilots who guided the rafts through the Conewago Falls made the White House their headquarters. It is estimated that upwards of one thousand rafts have been tied up in one day at this point. It was also a favorite rendezvous for the country youths on the Sabbath when they became apt students of the Yankees in gambling, drinking and profanity.

Highspire is a pleasant village, prominently known in later years for the excellent brand of "Spiritus Frumenti" produced here and the many charming homes that look out upon a beautiful stretch of river with the York hills for a background. It was called "Tinian" in Colonial days after the country seat of Colonel James Burd, a hero of the revolution, which stands on the hill back of the village, in full view of river and railroad. Colonel Burd built "Tinian" in 1763, the old stone house being well-preserved, the old-fashioned brass knocker remaining on the door at this day. John Hollingsworth built a mill here in 1775. It was burned in 1800, and another structure was erected on the site of the old one. The Wilson distillery was established here in 1823, its products reaching all parts of the globe. Beyond the town is Ulrich's woods, through which runs an avenue from east to west, and hedged on each side by small and larger trees, affording an unobstructed view to the river beyond. It is said Colonel Bouquet cut this road while marching to Bedford, although some attribute it to General Braddock.

Nearly two miles above one may see the trace of what was known as Chambers ferry, called Simpson's on the Cumberland side of the river. Colonel Simpson occupied a large stone house built upon the bluff, where he once entertained Washington and Lafayette on their way west. In 1807 Chambers and Simpson leased their ferries at $170 and $300, respectively. The road was much frequented by wagoners from the backwoods country who crossed the mountains at Sterret's Gap, reaching the Tuscarora Valley by way of Liberty Gap. Hawk Rock, a favorite fishing place is near Simpson's ferry.

Steelton, the most flourishing and substantial manufacturing town on the Susquehanna, had in 1866 a population of six families. To-day the population exceeds 10,000 souls. Its growth was phenomenal due solely to the location of the Pennsylvania Steel Works in the year previous mentioned. The land on which the original works were located was owned by Messrs Rudolph F. and Henry A. Kelker, and purchased from them by popular subscription among the business men of Harrisburg, amounting to $24,577.50. Other purchases have since been made by the company to accommodate their increased business. The town of Steelton proper was laid out by Rudolph F. Kelker, who sold only to those who intended to build. Subsequently speculators secured the land adjoining and the price of lots increased rapidly. The Pennsylvania Steel Works are leading manufacturers of steel in the United States, employing and giving steady labor to more than three thousand men. During the twenty-seven years that have passed since laying the foundation for its immense plant the company has experienced but one strike, 1891 when none of the departments were totally crippled, many of the employes refused to go out and in less than a week the strike was declared off. The policy of the company has always been marked by a generous and liberal treatment of its employes, the advancement of their moral and social relations and domestic happiness. The Steelton high school building, a magnificent structure containing ten school-rooms, exhibition hall and superintendent's room, was erected and presented to the borough school board free of all expense. A night visit to the Bessemers, rail-mills, blooming-mills, open-hearth furnaces, rolling-mills, frog and switch departments, blast furnaces, machine shops and numerous other industries will well repay all who indulge themselves.

RESCUE OF JOHN HARRIS.

BUT see! around the old man is that band!
Each tongue is mute, but stretched is every hand.
A shout uprose, each lip joins in the cry,
While vengeance flames in every flashing eye;
The old man, reflecting on the curse,
And all the evils that it brings for worse,
Refuses gently the request in tones
That meek humility only owns.
Quick as a flash of lightning from the sky
Rolls down the river bank the dreadful cry —
The stake! while from the hills there came
Echo's sound, till back is hurled the same.
Unmoved by threats the fearless old man stands,
Folded upon his breast his harmless hands;
"Indians," said he, "to thee I freely sell
The goods of life, but not the ills of hell;

Taste not the accursed draught 'twill prove to thee
Eternal death—eternal misery."
        Scarce had the words from his lips fell
Ere through the woodlands rung a loud, loud yell—
"Death to the trader!" burst in one wild cry,
But steady was the brave man's eye;
He feared not death, if duty found a grave,
And violated virtue must his save.

        Inflamed with rage, the red-browed race leaped up
Resolved to force from him the damning cup,
Seizing the bold old man, they rudely bore
His unresisting form along the shore;
He plead nor prayed to them, but smiled alone,
Pointing above to the great White Throne;
Foaming with wrath, beneath a primeval tree,
They bound his limbs to mark his agony,
But Harris saw beyond the verge of time
A power Omnipotent, a power sublime,
Who from his arms could rend the strongest chain,
And bid him rise unscathed again.

        Lashed to a tree, the Indians build a pyre,
And pile the fagots ready for a fire;
The blazing torch with shouts they now apply,
Shouts that run echoing thro' the vaulted sky
But still that good old man with peaceful gaze,
Beholds around the bursting blaze;
Nor heeds he now the dusky forms that there
Are waiting for the shrieks of his despair;
His pious spirit, at the crystal gates
Of heaven in faith for succor calmly waits.

        Wildly the dance of death begins; the flame
Like living vipers coils around his frame
But hark! from yonder woody shore there glide
Three bark canoes across the rapid tide;
The resentful Indians leap on shore to save
Their paleface "father" from a dismal grave
"Onward to save him," cries the brave young chief,
With gleaming knives they fly to his relief;
Back, back they drive the inebriated throng,
Who mad with frenzy, chant the wild death song
Severing the bonds which bound him to the tree,
Again beneath the heavens he stood free;
Unscathed was he and fearless still his eye,
For his souls trust was in his God on high,
And what is man if in that trust undone?—
His heart's a waste, a world without a sun.

                              ANDREW JACKSON HEER

HARRISBURG, THE CAPITAL CITY.

ARRISBURG, the gateway to Central Pennsylvania, and Capital of the State, is a beautiful city, located on an elevated plain or plateau, above the Susquehanna and fully twenty-five feet from low water mark. This plateau is in reality an immense island, oval in shape, and surrounded by the river, Paxton Creek and Fox's Run. Of recent years the city has overstepped the ancient boundary lines, reaching far into the adjoining townships. It embraces within its corporate limits 2,272 acres and has a population of 36,385. Since the centennial of its founding, an event duly celebrated in 1885, Harrisburg has experienced a marvelous growth, solid and substantial in general character, and encouraging to those having the real welfare of the city at heart. For generations and until long after the close of the rebellion, the State Capital wore a Van Winklean look and a frown of contempt for all innovations with tendencies to compel the old ways to reconstruct themselves and don the habiliments of progress, enterprise and municipal pride and ambition. For years Harrisburg bore the reputation of being the native heath of the "clam," a species of individual that will not move out of a given line, and opposes the fellow with push, pluck and vim who desires to do good for himself and those about him. But it is evidence of a greater and broader spirit of progress to note that the "clam" is being made use of, viz: to populate the handsome cemeteries that are in the vicinity.

The commercial advantages of Harrisburg are superior to all other rival cities, Philadelphia and Pittsburg excepted, railroads from every section of the country centering here, thus affording unexcelled advantages for the manufacture and shipment of iron and other products. The splendid railroad system radiating from it has been of especial importance to Harrisburg and made it a point of supplies for the merchant, the farmer and mechanic. The largest industrial establishments in the State are located here, and through all the years of financial stringency that threatened the prosperity of the country, they kept steadily on, disbursing thousands of dollars monthly to the working classes and aiding in the gradual building up of a great inland city. Harrisburg can well boast of her churches, schools, and banking institutions, factories, depots for supplies, railway connections, the finest hotels and electric street railways connecting all parts of the city with the neighboring towns.

John Harris, an Englishman, who originally settled in Chester county, built the first cabin in this locality. Like others of his day, he came to America to make money out of traffic with the Indians. Finding the banks of the Delaware uncongenial to his tastes and ambitions he pushed into the wilderness, stopping for a while at Bainbridge, then at the mouth of the Swatara, now Middletown. The precise date of Harris' arrival at Paxtang creek is not of record, but he is heard of prior to 1726, when he permanently located on the banks of the Susquehanna, at the point where Front and Paxton streets intersect. Here he built a log house, with extensive sheds, the whole surrounded by a high stockade. He traded with the Indians, exchanging goods of all kinds for furs. He married Esther Say, also a native of England, by whom he had one son, John Harris, Jr.

said to be the first white child born west of Conewago Falls. The lad was born in October, 1727, and was in the following September taken to Philadelphia on horseback for baptism. John Harris, before locating on the Susquehanna, laid the foundation of his wealth by pulling stumps from the streets in Philadelphia. Harris bought land, the title to which he did not obtain until 1733, adding by degrees to his purchase until he owned several hundred acres. He was as industrious as he was shrewd, combining agriculture with business pursuits to a successful degree, and did not scruple to sell whiskey and powder to the

Harrisburg from Fort Washington.

Indians, when he was not personally endangered thereby. He also accumulated money through the operation of what was known for a half century as "Harris' Ferry," that crossed the river from Paxton street to the old ferry house, the ruins of which are still standing below the end of the Cumberland Valley railroad bridge, at Bridgeport. Harris had a craving for more land, and squatted on Duncan's Island, but was forced to give them up on complaint from the Iroquois, through Chief Shikalamy. At one time, Harris narrowly escaped death at the stake, the Indians becoming enraged because of his refusal to give them more rum, of which he believed they had sufficient. He was tied to a mulberry tree and the fire already started, when some friendly Indians whose village was near West Fairview came to his rescue. A colored servant named Hercules, is said to have carried the news of his master's danger across the river, and was ever after held in high esteem by Harris and his family.

John Harris, the settler, died in 1748, and was buried beneath the old mulberry tree along the river bank. His grave is enclosed by an iron fence, a tombstone being placed therein with an appropriate inscription. For years the stump of the mulberry tree stood the action of the elements, but finally succumbed to the inevitable, the decayed remains being removed in 1889. The younger John Harris had been brought up beneath the eye of his father, whose business sagacity, courage and energy he inherited. He was married twice, the names of his wives being Elizabeth McClure and Mary Reed, respectively. Mary died in 1787. John Harris, Jr., on getting control of his estate, at once secured a legal right to operate the ferry, which continued to be a source of revenue for sixty years thereafter. He took part in all the Indian wars, leading several expeditions in person,

One of the first to declare for American Independence, he also loaned the government three thousand pounds. He had unbounded confidence in the future of Harris' Ferry. All his plans were based on what he believed was in store for the place, which also led him to lay out streets and avenues, and devise means whereby the seat of government might be transferred to the town yet in embryo. In 1785, when Harris laid out the town proper, three score houses already occupied sites near the river bank. Claiming the privilege of naming the town by reason of certain grants of land for public purposes, viz: Market Square and Capital Park, he christened it Harrisburg. After a dispute with the Supreme Court, who wanted the name "Louisburg" applied to point and the original choice, Harrisburg, it, Harris gained his was recognized in law. The large stone mansion at the corner of Front and Washington streets, the residence of the late General Simeon Cameron, was built by John Harris, Jr., in being completed in 1766, three years after starting the foundation. It was a pretentious building in its day, the possession of which made John Harris a man of prominence and influence among his less wealthy neighbors. Many readers who called upon General Cameron during his lifetime will recognize the elegant old mansion that bears such marked comparison with the old log house built by John Harris, Sr. The death of John Harris, Jr., occurred July 29, 1791. He was buried in the old Paxtang graveyard, the rest ing place of many old settlers of the Paxtang Valley. The Penns once offered Harris all the land from the west shore of the Susque

John Harris' Cabin, Grave and House of Harris the Second.

hanna, including the site of Indian villages, at West Fairview and New Cumberland, as far up as Silver's Spring, and extending across the Cumberland Valley from mountain to mountain, for $25,000. Harris tendered them $17,500, and refused to give more. The Indian wars between 1750 and 1765, created great excitement at Harris' Ferry, and not until the march of the Paxtang Boys on Conestoga and subsequent annihilation of the tribe did the settlers feel safe from slaughter. In 1790 the feeling in Congress toward making Harrisburg the Federal seat of government was so strong that the vote at one time was a tie. The Legislature, in February, 1842, passed an act authorizing the removal of all the State officers from Lancaster to Harrisburg, which was the decisive step in this direction. The corner-stone of the Capitol was laid May 31, 1819, and was completed 1821, since which time many additions and improvements have been made. Visitors to the Capital City will not go away without indulging in a stroll through the beautiful park and a thorough inspection of the State buildings. The Capital stands on a handsome, sloping elevation, affording an excellent view of the surroundings. The grounds are tastefully laid out in gravel walks and drive-ways winding among the tall, umbrageous trees of vigorous growth and broad shade. Along the public promenades, placed at convenient distances, are benches where one may rest and enjoy the beauties about him. Two artificial fountains, with rustic centers, occupy prominent positions near the buildings. A smaller statue fountain, "The Unfortunate Boy," a recent addition to the Park attractions, is a great favorite with the children. Then there is the stately Mexican Monument erected to the memory of Pennsylvanians who lost their lives during the Mexican War. It is surrounded by a fence composed of flint-lock muskets that were carried from the Rio Grande to the very doors of the Montezumas. At the foot of the monument, placed on a huge frame, are a number of Mexican cannon captured by the Pennsylvania troops.

The conservatory, where flowers bloom as profusely in December as May, is a fine building of unique design and convenient appointments. The numerous entrances to the Park have lately been beautified by elaborately carved steps and balustrades that show their massive grandeur to

Governor, R. E. Pattison.

excellent advantage. The visitor will not forget to look into the Senate Chamber and Hall of the House of Representatives before ascending to the second story. Here are apartments for the State Library containing 97,000 volumes, in charge of Dr. William H. Egle, a distinguished historian, antiquarian and general writer.

Capitol Buildings.

offices of the Attorney General, Superintendent of Public Instruction, Adjutant General and Lieutenant Governor. The Flag-Room, the depository of the battle-torn banners carried by the Pennsylvania Regiments during the late war between the States, is a most sacred shrine where those who wore the Blue and fought to defend the glorious stars and stripes may direct their footsteps and gaze in silent veneration upon the precious relics.

After all the years that intervene
    Between the fall of Sumpter and to-day,
        The faded banners, torn and old,
        Have tales of comfort yet untold,
    And patriotism marks each fold
Though death holds lips at bay.

With hearts most grateful, tenderest words,
And lashes pearled with honest tears,
Gaze on the ragged flags! No blot
Or tarnish to the sight is brought,
But noble, faithful duties taught
By lessons from those years.

Captive Guns.

God bless the flags! Their records bright
Add glory to the righteous cause;
Freedom won a new birthright
And reverence for her laws.
Guard them, O men, to whom is given
The guidance of our State!
Emblems of valor born of heaven,
Defying shafts by traitors driven,—
Protect them! Lowly,—great.

To the south of the main building is the office of the Secretary of Internal Affairs, containing also the Supreme Court Chamber. The north building shown in the engraving, is occupied by the Auditor General, State Treasurer, and on the second story by the Secretary of State and the Governor of the Commonwealth, Hon. Robert E. Pattison. The Executive Department is much visited by strangers and open to all persons, to whom is shown the most courteous attention by the Governor and those about him. On the walls of the reception-room hang the portraits of all the Governors of Pennsylvania, from the adoption of the Constitution of 1790 down to and including the present incumbent, who was elected in 1882 and again in 1890. The Governor's mansion is on Front street near State.

From the dome of the Capitol one may behold a landscape unexcelled for variety of effects, picturesque beauty and charming river scenery. To the north are the famous Kittatinny mountains called by the Indians "The Endless Hills," and Rockville Gap, through which flows the Susquehanna. Looking in the same direction the eye cannot

On the River Near Harrisburg

miss the great white dome that crowns the Lunatic Hospital, opened for the reception of patients in 1851. Turning to the East one may see the State Arsenal, a splendid building for the storage of military supplies; the Harrisburg Cemetery where repose the remains of three of Pennsylvania's Governors, viz: William Findlay, 1817-1820; David R. Porter, 1839-1845; and John W. Geary, 1867-1873. Distant a few lots from the tomb of the latter, is the grave of the first Joseph Jefferson, grandfather of the present distinguished actor of Rip Van Winkle celebrity; Prospect Park the location of the city reservoir which prominently extends eastward and forms the historic Paxtang Valley. To the South is Steelton and the York hills that blend into the South mountain range and at whose feet lie cultivated farms, cosy homes and the growing town of New Cumberland. Looking westward is the far-famed Cumberland Valley, where the hardy and intrepid Scotch-Irish early made homes and secured valuable estates. Here flows the broad Susquehanna about whose shores cluster richest memories interspersed with traditionary lore, nineteenth century progress and the magic of homely and familiar associations. There are the green isles that everywhere break the otherwise monotony of a wide expanse of water, the rippling waves dancing beneath the sunlight and coquetting with nodding trees and grass-fringed shore. Then too there comes to the ear a welcome sound from the multitudes in the streets below that tells of the ebbing and flowing of humanity's tides, of earnest competition in trades, professions and business circles; of the joys and pleasures sought after in the pursuit of man's gratifications. Fortune and of burdens that fret and bear heavily down upon weary shoulders that ache with the toils of the day.

Four bridges span the river at Harrisburg, two of which are used for vehicles and foot travel exclusively. The first bridge to be built across the Susquehanna at this point and widely-known as "The Old Camel Back Bridge." It was finished in 1816, nearly four years being consumed in its construction. The builder was Theodore Burr, and the price paid him $480,000, of which sum the State appropriated $80,000. The part next to Front street was carried away by the flood of March 15, 1846, and rebuilt in 1847. It was destroyed by fire in 1866 and again rebuilt in the year following. The bridge running between the island and Cumberland shore is the original Burr plan, said to be the only one of the kind in the world. It is a rare curiosity. The State's share of stock, $80,000, was sold to private parties for $9,000. The Cumberland Valley railroad bridge was built and opened for travel at 2.30 p. m., January 16, 1839. The first train leaving Bridgeport was composed of two baggage cars, three coaches, and the locomotive, "Nicholas Biddle." It was destroyed by fire in 1844 and immediately rebuilt. This structure was supplanted by another in 1859 and this again by the present iron bridge, completed in 1886. The South Penn Railroad

Company contracted for a bridge across the river at Paxton street, the piers of which were erected in the summer of 1885. The road was never completed and the piers are pointed out as "The Vanderbilt monuments." The People's bridge, at Walnut street, was built by popular subscription in 1889 and designed as a rival of the "Old Camelback." They were consolidated during the present year. The handsome iron bridge crossing the River at Paxton street was built by the Philadelphia and Reading Company in 1890, and is parallel with the South Penn piers. There are many other points of interest

Fishing—Opposite McCormick's Island.

in and around Harrisburg worthy of special visit, the convenience afforded by the electric street cars running on the principal streets being ample for all requirements or purposes. The close proximity of the Kittatinny and South mountain ranges, the numerous groves popular with the people as pleasure resorts, and the facilities for reaching the same conspire toward making a residence at the Capital City one of enjoyment and desirability.

There is a stretch of river, from Harrisburg to Rockville, that is worthy of a passing notice. Taking the turnpike, or as it is known to pleasure seekers, "The River Road," one may behold a five-mile panorama of scenery unsurpassed in loveliness and beauty of landscape. The drive is a delightful one and will linger long among the happy experiences of life. McCormick's Island, a large, fertile tract of land in mid-river, is popular as a picnic resort. In the vicinity of the Island the choicest terrapin are found. Estherton is the name of a roadside village, better known as "Coxestown," and was prominent in ante-revolution times. It was laid out in 1762, by Dr. John Cox, of Philadelphia. Farther on is a relic of ye olden times, the homestead of the Otts. The old mansion was built in 1764, the brick used in its first construction being brought from Philadelphia. It was partially destroyed by fire and afterwards remodeled. In the early part of the present century the old house had the reputation of being the rendezvous of thieves and counterfeiters who plied their nefarious trade among rivermen and wagoners on the Pittsburg and Philadelphia turnpike, passing the door. A tunnel was built connecting the house with the river, but all traces have disappeared. The scenery at Rockville, where the Pennsylvania railroad crosses the Susquehanna, is the finest in the country. Rockville Gap possesses an historic charm to every admirer of Nature and homely associations. On the top of the mountain peak, whose steep sides extend down into the village, are the ruins of an old fort called by the settlers the "Indian Fort Hunter." From its rocky walls a sweeping view of the river in both directions may be obtained. It was one of the favorite retreats for Indians when on the war-path. Spencer Park is the home of 'Squire James McAllister, a genial companion and prominent citizen. He is a descendant of the McAllisters who settled at Fort Hunter.

OUR RIVER.

SENTINELED by mountains purple flows the river on its way,
Legends from the land of shadows whisper of a bygone day,
Races vanished and forgotten lived and loved upon its shore,
And its placid rippling waters have been stained with deepest gore.

It has heard the din of carnage, seen the bitter, deadly strife,
On its banks of fairest beauty has been born a broader life.
Darts the light came no longer over its waters, calm and clear,
And no savage storm and vengeful wakens now the white man's fear.

Solemn secrets holds the river in its ever silent breast—
Secrets of the buried ages and of nations laid to rest.
Wooded hills and lonely islands may no knowledge now impart,
Swells the storied wealth of ages deep within the river's heart.

Flow its waters on, unceasing, tireless, restless, swift and fast,
While its current gives no token of the cruel, heartless past.
This, the lesson that it teacheth: Look not at the withered sod,
Live but in the present moment, Live and work for man and God!

1897.   MABEL CRONISE JONES.

CAMP CURTIN.

AMP Curtin is of the past. Its name and memories live but in the recollections of those who fought for the Union, or in the magic dream life of the present generation, then too young to realize the horrors and demoralization of war, and who now draw upon history, written and verbal, for a more comprehensive and familiar idea of the memorable conflict. The story of Camp Curtin may be told briefly, its origin, uses and final abandonment, though volumes might be written to enrich the literature of romance and realism to an almost unlimited extent.

During war times Harrisburg, besides being the Capital of Pennsylvania, that had so conspicuously declared the Union shall and must be preserved, thus practically and fearlessly leading in the movement to defend the United States from its enemies and home-born traitors, was centrally located on the great railway whose branches and connections ramified and touched the entire country

Old Camp Curtin Hospital.

west of the Alleghenies and north of the Empire State line. In addition to these advantages, the then young Governor, Andrew G. Curtin, inaugurated January 15, 1861, had declared openly and enthusiastically for the abolition of slavery, and from which position he never surrendered through all the years of conflict following. It is said of him that he came to the Executive Chair just as hostilities were opening, and he occupied it until the smoke of the conflict had cleared away, and the veterans from many a hard-fought field and lonely bivouac, with banners streaming in triumph, came marching home.

When war became inevitable Governor Curtin issued his famous call for volunteers, out of which was formed the celebrated Pennsylvania Reserve Corps that so signally distinguished itself throughout the rebellion. By the massing of large bodies of men at the State Capital Governor Curtin saw at once the necessity of providing a place of rendezvous where the recruits could be properly drilled and disciplined. It was then—April, 1861,—that the fields north of the city were leased and immediately occupied. The ground selected was above the Asylum road, at that time nearly a mile beyond the limits, or built-up portions of the city. The location was considered perfect. The limits of the camp, from a present survey, included all the land bounded by Watts lane on the north, the Pennsylvania railroad on the east, Asylum road, or Maclay street, on the south, and what is now known as Fifth street on the west. Captain Doyel Unger was the owner of most all the land so occupied. Here the tents were pitched in rows, forming a white village of canvas covering acres of green-sward that soon became trampled and bared by the thousands of passing feet. It was soon deemed necessary to erect a hospital for the accommodation of the sick and wounded, the latter being sent from the front or taken ill en route to their homes on furlough. The illustration is an excellent likeness of the hospital building, the site of which was, until recently, occupied by the farm belonging to St. Genevieve's Academy. To the hospital came the noble women of Harrisburg to care for the sick and minister to their wants. They indulged in their charitable and kindly duties with a willingness and fortitude never excelled, and seldom equaled. They distinguished themselves for kindness and self-sacrificing devotion to the health, cheerfulness and comfort of the soldier, rendering efficient aid, both in the sick wards and in the camp. Verily, they shall have their reward. An appropriate, though brief, synopsis of woman's experience in the wards of the hospital is told with truth and pathos in the lines following, and written by a Southerner:

WOMAN'S WAR MISSION.

"Look around!" By the torchlight unsteady
　　The dead and the dying seem one—
What, paling and trembling already,
　　Before your dear mission's begun?

Pause here by this bedside—how mellow
　　The light showers down on that brow—
Such a brave, brawny visage—Poor fellow,
　　Some homestead is missing him now.

Some wife shades her eyes in the clearing,
　　Some mother sits moaning—distressed,
While the loved one lies faint, but uncaring,
　　With the enemy's ball in his breast.

Here's another, a lad—a mere stripling—
　　Picked up from the field almost dead;
With the blood through his sunny hair rippling
　　From a horrible gash in the head.

Fought and fell 'neath the guns of that city,
　　With a spirit transcending his years,
Lift him up in your large-hearted pity
　　And touch his pale lips with your tears.

Pass on. It is useless to linger,
    While others are claiming your care;
There is need of your delicate finger,
    For your womanly sympathy there.

There are sick ones athirst for caressing,
    There are dying ones raving of home;
There are wounds to be bound with a blessing,
    And shrouds to make ready for some.

They have gathered about you the harvest
    Of death, in its ghastliest view;
The nearest as well as the farthest
    Is here with the traitor and true.

And crowned with your beautiful patience,
    Made sunny with love at the heart,
You must balsam the wounds of a nation,
    Nor falter, nor shrink from your part.

I grant that the task's superhuman,
    But strength will be given to you
To do for those dear ones what woman
    Alone, in her pity can do.

But e'en if you drop down unheeded,
    What matter? God's ways are the best;
You've poured out your life where 'twas needed,
    And he will take care of the rest."

A daily witness of the most stirring scenes, Harrisburg, happily for its inhabitants, experienced none of the disastrous scenes consequent upon the capture and occupation by the dreaded foe. Located on the Susquehanna, it was the key to communications with Washington and the entire North. Believing in its strength to resist the approach of the Confederate army, it became the objective point of Southern refugees and the inhabitants of the border counties. Little apprehension was manifested until June, 1863, when the daring and still bolder movements of the foe caused a feeling of anxiety to pervade even Camp Curtin itself. It was in the dawn of the month of roses when the Confederate army, flushed with the pride of two victories—Fredericksburg and Chancellorsville—that Lee, in emulation of Alexander, thought of weeping because he found there were no more foes to conquer. A commander of his disposition could not remain long idle, and consequently backed by the government at Richmond, preparations were hurriedly made to move North. Lee knew that a lodgment on Pennsylvania soil, be it ever so dangerous, meant a great deal from a military standpoint, and cherished a hope that Pennsylvania's Capital would fall into his hands. Besides, the advance, if successful, could not fail of restoring confidence among the supporters of Jefferson Davis, who, at different periods, doubted the wisdom of Lee's actions. It was Lee's ambition and desire to transfer the theater of war to the east of the Susquehanna, knowing too well the effect upon the country at large were such results attained. The State Capital became thoroughly alarmed at the report of Lee's advance, and was followed by Governor Curtin's proclamation of June 12, assuring the people of the impending danger and urging them to enlist and organize for self-protection. General Couch was busy at Camp

Curtin mustering in and having drilled the constantly increasing ranks, and making preparations for a stubborn resistance. The citizens organized themselves into companies and were at once assigned for duty. The contents of the State Library, together with all valuable State papers were shipped to Philadelphia; fortifications were thrown up in Harris Park and at other points along Front street; citizens volunteered to work on the hill opposite Harrisburg, now known as "Fort Washington," where a long line of breastworks soon crowned the summit, and from which could be seen the glitter of cannon and musketry ready to greet the invading army that did not come. Those were days of anxiety in Harrisburg, and when Carlisle fell into the enemy's power, the excitement became intense. Regiment after regiment left Camp Curtin for points in the Cumberland Valley, where the Confederate General was having things his own way, and others but awaited orders to march off. During the afternoon of June 29th, the Confederates had advanced as far as Oyster's Point, four miles west of Harrisburg, on the Carlisle pike, where a skirmish took place. General Knipe was in command of the home troops. The enemy was pushing on toward the Susquehanna when Knipe turned upon them the guns of Miller's Battery which soon forced them to retreat. Oyster's Point was, therefore, the nearest advance to Harrisburg of the enemy in force. To prevent the approach of the Confederates spans of the "Old Camel-Back" bridge were severed, ready to be dropped into the river in case an attempt were made to cross. With a knowledge of the shallowness of the Susquehanna at that season of the year, when one can almost walk from shore to shore upon the rocky bottom, the sawing of the bridge spans seems ridiculous. On the morning of June 30th all signs of the raiders had vanished in the direction of Gettysburg where the great battle was fought July 1, 2 and 3. Thereafter the State Capital was not molested by Confederates or rumors of Confederates until the war closed in '65.

The first volunteer military company to reach Harrisburg in response to Governor Curtin's call for troops was the Ringgold Artillery, of Reading, arriving at eight p. m. April 16th. The Logan Guards, of Lewistown, arrived the next morning. They left for Washington April 18th with few guns and no uniforms. Enlistment rapidly followed until the tent line of Camp Curtin was extended; quarters for the men increased, and provisions every way enlarged to meet the growing demands, made so by the echo of Anderson's guns at Fort Sumpter reverberating in the ears of the patriots of the North. The last tent was removed from Camp Curtin in September, 1865, though traces of the famous ground remained for years after. By and by Harrisburg began growing westward, progress and population reaching out toward the Asylum Road and embracing the territory between the river and railroad. Year by year these changes increased until at length a village site was laid out on the very spot marked by the imprint of tent-poles. Like pilgrims to a sacred shrine the veterans come back for a farewell look at old scenes but find so little to remind them of war days. They are waiting the final reveille when they shall be mustered in for eternity. The land marks are all gone; the last to disappear was the old pump. It is now a sacred relic in the museum of Post 58, College Block; a gift from Colonel John Motter, who owned the ground where the well was filled up. The site of the well is opposite Grace's Hotel. To recall the changes that have gradually crept into the vicinity of Camp Curtin one has but to look back a dozen years. Then Asylum road was considered an out of the way place. Few houses were built above Harris street and cultivated fields greeted the eye long before the Stock Yard Hotel was reached. But time has changed all this. On old Camp Curtin a village has been built and homes for the working man founded. Where the roll of the drums, the gruff call of the sentry and the hum of a populous camp sounded, now twenty-eight years peace rules; industry thrives and prosperity shares alike with all.

A RIVER REVERIE.

As twilight chases the sunset behind the mountain's brow,
As night steals o'er the valley and the life of the day is low,
I loose my boat from its moorings and float on the placid stream,
Out into the gathering darkness, into a sleepless dream.

The weird wash of the water on the river's pebbled shore,
The mellowed rush of the ripple and the quiet dip of the oar
Are sounds that break the silence, so lonely, gloomy yet grand,
That hangs like a dusky curtain 'twixt the sky and the dark'ning land.

As I float, with trailing paddle past islands growing dim,
I hear the vespers chiming the notes of a sweet old hymn;
A hymn that brings recollections of life's most sunny days,
And I lose myself in fancy till the real becomes a maze.

I pass where the lights of the city shine out from the ghost-like shore,
The clock in the State-House tower tells the hour gone before;
The distant hills of Cumberland stand forth in their lonesomeness
And guard-like faithful sentries, the river we praise and bless.

The cheering noise of factory, the furnace's hum and glow
Are Labor's grandest chorus ever heard by man below;
And I float with bated breathing, with silent lip and tongue—
The melody is not forgotten, though the song remains unsung.

My boat drifts with the current 'neath bridges frowning and low,
Away from the busy city into the night unknown,
Till I rouse from my happy reverie, and with stroke of trusty oar
The boat drifts swiftly shoreward, and I live in the real once more.

ZENAS J. GRAY.

OLD FORT HUNTER.

On the east bank of the Susquehanna at the mouth of Fishing Creek, opposite the town of Marysville, and six miles above Harrisburg, is Old Fort Hunter, a name spoken and known for more than one hundred and fifty years. There are no traces of the old-time battlements, no rusty cannon—nothing to indicate the part this famous locality figured in the struggle for settlement and civilization of the Susquehanna and Juniata Valleys. Yet it is Old Fort Hunter! Old in local history and story, in colonial and ante-Revolutionary records and traditions that have come down through verbal and historic highways.

Fort Hunter was one of the earliest settlements west of the Conestoga, and soon became noted for its frontier advantages as a place of rendezvous and defense and supply station for other posts farther up and beyond the Susquehanna. Numerous conferences with the Indians were held here, nearly all of which but proved the craftiness and treachery of their race. Prior to 1730, one Joseph Chambers, with three brothers, took possession of three hundred acres of land and built thereon a large double cabin, and the first grist-mill above the Swatara. The mill was of logs, primitive in appearance, but it fulfilled its mission. It was patronized by the settlers from the Paxtang Valley and those as far west as Duncan's Island, who brought their corn and wheat to be made into flour. The original building was washed away by the log flood of 1784, since which two mills have been built on or near the old site. Chambers's place was the resort for Indians, settlers, traders and adventurers of all classes, the jovial disposition of the owner and the plain, honest hospitality dispensed soon attracted a large patronage. The batteauxmen, who did a thriving business on the river, and who tied up at Fort Hunter, were, according to the Journal of the Rev. David Brainerd, an English missionary, who, in 1746, stopped at Chambers' over night, "an ungodly crew who drank rum" and indulged in unlimited profanity. About the year 1755 the Provincial government ordered the erection of a line of forts at certain points on the east bank of the Susquehanna. Chambers' was the first to be selected, and the high bluff facing, and extending into the river, was considered the most eligible. It was advantageous from a military standpoint, the embankment being more than thirty feet above the river and overlooking it as far as McCormick's Island on the south and great bend, beyond Dauphin, on the north. Fort Hunter was not built for strong defense and could not have withstood a sudden or determined attack from the enemy had one been made. Originally it was a long, low building of logs used for garrison purposes, surrounded by an entrenchment supported by stones at the parapet bases. Eight years after its erection Rev. John Elder wrote Governor Hamilton that the earth-works were level with the ground and called his attention to the absolute necessity of having erected "a stockade to cover the men."

In 1785 Chambers sold his land including the old fort and tavern to Archibald McAllister, who was a typical boniface of ye olden time. His establishment was the gathering place of the entire neighborhood, the guests numbering among them boatmen, wagoners, travelers from the far away Alleghenies and the rich speculators from the East, all of whom doubtless enjoyed their stay.

In 1811 few traces of the old fort were visible, and later the large mansion house standing near the edge of the precipitous bank was built. The property is now in the possession of the D. D. Boas estate, of Harrisburg. In the large lawn are several relics of pioneer days—trees, tall, majestic and of immense girth, whose genial shade has cooled the brows of many generations.

KITTATINNY.

NOR mount sublime, nor humblest one of all,
    Thy gentle beauty, ever brought to mind,
    Turns thought to thee with every mild wind
      In woods of thine resounds the pheasant's call,
      And nimble squirrels chirp from treetops tall;
    Thy ozone-laden airs the senses bind,
    And nature adds the smallest of its kind,
A musically tinkling waterfall
When morning's brilliant sunlight gilds thy crest,
    And night's dark mists are rolled back to the sky—
While fragrant flowers nestle on thy breast,
    And with the fern leaves to adorn thee, vie—
Thy mantle blue, with glistening dewdrops drest,
    Clothes nature's queen and heaven's joy on high.

                           JOHN HANDIBOE.

ROCKVILLE TO DUNCANNON.

OVER the magnificent iron bridge, the traveler is rapidly carried into the heart of the famous gap that takes its name from the town situated at the eastern end of the bridge. The latter is 3,670 feet in length above the point known to raftsmen as "Wenzel's Nose." Three miles further on is Marysville, once a thriving and industrious town, before the abandonment by the Northern Central Railway of the bridge, the piers of which are still noticeable. The scenery here is wild, the Kittatinny Mountains on the east and the Tuscarora on the west, forming a foreground picturesque to a remarkable degree. The river is broken by the rapids called "Hunter's Falls," the site of old Fort Hunter being opposite. Huge rocks abound, through which the current dashes and surges, and was ever the fear and dread of the rivermen. Dauphin is on the opposite shore, in Dauphin county. It is a desirable place of residence in summer. Passing around the end of the mountain, you are in the Cove, a celebrated locality and a great favorite with Harrisburgers, many of whom own handsome cottages where they spend vacation days and entertain friends. The Cove is a geological peculiarity. Prof. Claypole says its physical features are entirely due to the presence and direction of the Pocono Sandstone Mountain, which crosses the river at Duncannon under the name of Peter's or Fourth Mountain, runs to the southwest, then curves around and turning eastward at the Horseshoe returns to the Susquehanna River, which it crosses above Marysville. The Cove is considered the western extremity of the southern angle of the

Rockville Gap—Looking Up Stream.

great Pottsville coal basin. The river, after passing through the gap at Duncannon, flows slantingly down and across the Cove, five miles, turns in through a gap in the Second Mountain at Marysville and Dauphin, thence through the Rockville gap towards Harrisburg. The fall of the Susquehanna through the Cove is estimated at 1.58 feet per mile, from the Cove to Rockville, 2.60, thence to Harrisburg the rate is 1.35 feet. From Mahantongo, above Liverpool to Rockville, a distance of 30¼ miles, the river has a total fall of 81½ feet, or at the rate of 2¼ feet per mile. The several falls, or rapids which are frequently referred to, form natural dams, over which the river has been tumbling for ages. The conclusion to be reached is that these natural dams must have been higher above the ocean level in each preceding age, following the process of wear and tear backwards, and the whole country from the Blue or Kittatiny Mountains at Rockville westward, was one great lake. There is ample evidence to prove this geological assertion.

Cove Forge Fish House in Winter.

The railroad company has made extensive improvements in the Cove that had much to do with its present popularity as a summer resort. At Cove Forge, a station east of Duncannon, the Harrisburg Fishing Club has elegant quarters. The club house stands on an eminence, three hundred feet above the river, and overlooking the entire Cove. It is a delightful resort in summer, and a place of rest at all seasons.

Duncannon is the busiest town in Perry county. For years it has enjoyed the distinction of being the manufacturing center of the river valley, as between Harrisburg and Lewistown. The Duncannon Iron Company owns and operates a furnace, rolling and nail mills. It is a prosperous town and is in direct communication by railway with the richest part of the country. East of town there is a spur of mountain called "Profile Rock," from its resemblance to the human face. On Sherman's Creek, not far from Duncannon the first settlements were made against the wishes of the Provincial Government, who sought to keep faith with the Indians. Col. Croghan, then a

resident of Carlisle, and after whom Sterritt's Gap was first named, was sent into Sherman's Valley to dispossess the settlers. He burned their cabins, laid waste their lands, and drove them from the valley.

Clarke's Ferry is so well known to all Pennsylvanians that a description of the locality might seem superfluous to those so informed, but its proximity to Duncannon and the close relation it bears to Duncan's Island and the mouth of the Juniata, is ample apology for any extended reference here. The ferry, or fording-place, was used as early as 1735 by the whites

Down the River From Duncannon.

who were pushing their way into the Juniata Valley. The river was easily crossed, the current being sluggish and not deep. The Indians called it "Queenashawkee." The river is three-fourths of a mile wide and is crossed by a wooden bridge. There is a double towing path built on the lower side used for towing boats, the channel changing from the east to the west bank. The dam is immediately below the bridge. It is a beautiful sheet of water and

forms a pool extending more than a mile above. There are fine fishing grounds below the dam, and are prolific of fish. The Bonvenue Club House is situated at the mouth of the Juniata on the Perry county shore. It is a charming site. The building is of stone, two stories high, the interior being commodious and convenient. It was formerly the old Paskin tavern and homestead. Facing the confluence of the Juniata and Susquehanna the river view is unequaled in placid

Bonvenue Club House.

beauty. The roar and sparkle of the waters as they fall over the conduit Clarke's Dam exert a delightful influence on the beholder, and but adds to the perspective with Peter's mountain towering high above and overlooking the historic neighborhood.

Duncan's Island at the junction of the two rivers, and a sister Island, Haldeman's, occupy the foremost position historically of the many famous localities west of Conestoga. Duncan's Island is perhaps the most noted, as it was the site of an Indian village, believed to have been "Atrakomi," first heard of in 1654. It is probable that it was occupied by the earliest tribes and maintained by them as a wayside place of rest and for the excellent fishing the two rivers furnished. Captain John Smith, when he explored the lower Susquehanna in 1608, was told by the Indians whom he met of the village, "Cheoniady," and Isaac Taylor, the Chester county surveyor, in 1701, made a map of the Susquehanna, on which he has marked, at the mouth of a large stream, "Choniaty." It was on Haldeman's Island, at what was known as "White Rock," that John Harris in 1733 built a cabin and sought to trade with the Indians but was forced to vacate. The Hulings and Watts were the earliest settlers on Duncan's Island, the former locating on the upper end in 1755. It, it was who established the ferry over the Juniata and built a causeway over the narrow stream near the present Aqueduct for pack-horses to pass over. Another settler named Baskin was the originator of what is still known as Clark's Ferry. During the Indian wars the settlers on the Juniata suffered extremely. In 1760 the Hulings' family was driven away. Placing his wife and child on the family horse, Hulings directed them to proceed to the point where the two rivers meet and await his coming. He went back to get a farewell shot, but was detained longer than expected, whereupon Mrs. Hulings became alarmed and forced the animal into the river through which he carried her in safety. She awaited her husband's arrival on the other side, and, together with a Mrs. Berryhill, whose husband was killed, they reached Fort Hunter. Rev. David Brainerd, in 1745 visited the Island, remaining several days at each visit. His description of the Indians and their mode of worship and manner of living is given with sincere regret at his inability to improve their conditions. A Mrs. Baskin, one of the original families, and two children were carried away by Indians. The boy escaped before leaving the Island, and Mrs. Baskin also eluded her captors near Carlisle. The daughter was taken to Ohio, where after six years of captivity she was returned to friends. She married a man named Smith and resided at Newport until her death. Duncan's Island was the favorite home of the Indians. Their burying ground was where the canal lock is now located. A great mound existed, out of which was taken large quantities of bones, implements made of stone and various trinkets. The Duncans inherited the island from their grandparents, the original Hulings and Watts who had inter-married. It is related of Hulings that in 1756 he owned two hundred acres at the mouth of the Juniata and was of the belief that a great city would spring up there. He moved to the junction of the Allegheny and Monongahela where he also took up land. Thinking the latter was too far west for profit he sold it, returning to his Island on the Susquehanna. One of his purchases is now Pittsburg, and the other Benevue. Although the old Duncan plantation still retains the name "Island" it is not in reality an island now. Before the construction of the canal the Juniata flowed into the Susquehanna, or vice versa, through a channel north of the Island, near Reutter's old tavern, and called by location, "the Gut." During the great flood of 1846 the embankment was swept out and the Susquehanna resumed its old course and rebuilt. The channel that surrounds Haldeman's Island is deep and rapid. It rejoins the river at Clarke's bridge.

ON THE BRIDGE WHERE THE RIVERS MEET

YEARS ago when the wind was low
    And the east was dim and grey,
And the west was red with the sunset glow,
    And the daylight ebbed away,
And never a sound came through the night
    Save the rush of the waters fleet
I stood where I stand in the waning light
    On the bridge where the rivers meet.

The years have come and the years have gone
    And have left their marks on me;
But the river unchanged speeds gaily on
    To the ever-changing sea,
The hills are unaltered far and near
    And the still scene is complete,
I alone seem changed who linger here
    On the bridge where the rivers meet.

                                    CHARLES JOHNS.

— —•—

SUNSET AT BENVENUE.

BELOW the bridge at sunset
    We take our rapid way
The oars are dipping lightly
    As if in merry play.

In the eddy twirling eddies
    The foamy waves flow on
Past many an enchanted island
    Bathed in the setting sun.

The waters, falling gently,
    Send up a misty spray
All brilliant with the beauty
    Of the fading day.

Across the lonely ferry
    From out the bridge's gloom
Away from the mountain's shadow
    The twilight colors come.

                                    EMMA F. CARPENTER.

INGLENOOK.

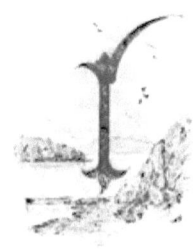

INGLENOOK, one of the most charming family resorts on the Susquehanna, is situated on the East bank, near Powell's creek, at the base of Peter's mountain, and about one and one-half miles above Clarke's Ferry dam. The grounds lie between the river and the Northern Central railroad, and is a recognized station at which all local trains stop. It is owned by a number of gentlemen representatives of prominent Harrisburg families, who, in 1888, organized themselves into an association for pleasure and social purposes, with necessary charter rights and privileges. The site is one of the prettiest north of Benvenue, and excellent judgment was displayed in its selection. There are two buildings of Queen Anne design, the largest of which is for the exclusive use and occupancy of the members, their families and invited guests. The interior is conveniently arranged and furnished to gratify the simpler desires of those that long for a genuine outing, with complete freedom from worldly cares, as well as others more luxuriously inclined. A large, old-fashioned fireplace, from which the resort takes its name, is the most conspicuous idolized object among the interior appointments. It is fitted up with

andirons, shovel and long tongs; and when the big hearth is piled high with blazing logs, the warmth and glow and cheerful surroundings throw over one a facinating

Inglenook—River View from Piazza.

spell out of which the awakening is accompanied by regrets. The poetic Ingleside of Scotland, made world-famous by the genius and songs of Robert Burns, finds a faithful and honored counterpart at High-rock-on-the-Susquehanna. The smaller cottage is the home of the steward, who has sole charge of the grounds and the cuisine.

The scenery is ravishingly beautiful, the variety and pleasing effects being unsurpassed. The main building stands by the shore and has for its foreground a broad, bewitching expanse of river nearly a mile wide. In appearance it is one vast lake, with a wild sweep of current that, washing the eastern bank, turns at right angles and runs direct to the farther shore. The boating is excellent, and the knights of the rod and gun can find both pleasure and game in return for their labors.

THE LAND BETWEEN THE RIVERS.

LET those who will as pilgrims go
    To climes across the ocean,—
I love the scenes which long ago
    Awaked my young emotion;
That bade my youthful thoughts arise,
    And manhood's high endeavors, —
My native home, that smiling lies,—
    The land between the rivers.

Though there no lordly castle throws
    O'er moor, or plain its shadow;
From where the Susquehanna flows
    Through mountain-gap and meadow,
To where the Juniata's tide
    Its tribute wave delivers —
The streams that bound on either side—
    The land between the rivers.

And spreads our river broad, a lake,
    With ceaseless currents fretting,
A thousand islands green that break
    The crystal of their setting;
And there the wildfowl gayly swim,
    And there the sunlight quivers,
Till evening veils with mantle dim
    The land between the rivers.

The purple mists of early morn
    With diadems of glory
Our rugged mountain crests adorn,
    Unknown to song or story.
And mountain-footed in golden light,
    They look where sways and quivers,
The water-lily's spotless white
    That grows beside the rivers.

SUSQUEHANNA AND JUNIATA RIVERS.

And soft in beauty sweetly lie
　　Our fertile vales extended,
Afar, where golden clouds on high,
　　And gold-green earth is blended:
No eye can trace the faint drawn line
　　Which hill and sky discovers;
So close the heavens bend down to join
　　The land between the rivers

And there, in sunset's dying day,
　　Through evening's sapphire portals,
Bright forms Angelic countless stray
　　Unseen by eyes of mortals:
Charmed from their fair celestial home,
　　Where Death ne'er comes nor severs,
To bless a second Eden's bloom
　　In land between the rivers.

　　　　　　　　　　G. CARY THEAT.

THE SUSQUEHANNA AT HALIFAX.

SWEET Riverview! Sweet Riverview!
　　I love thy hills and mountains blue,
　　Thy waters broad and sparkling bright
　　Their purple gleams of sunset light

　　Sweet Riverview! Sweet Riverview!
　　I love thy beauties, old and new;
　　I've found it here, though long the quest:—
　　Sweet peace of mind and perfect rest.

　　　　　　　　　　SARAH B. McFARLAND.

HALIFAX TO SELINSGROVE.

THERE may be a pleasure in the pathless woods," but the path ought not to lead one too far from home and friends. There is, however, a greater and safer pleasure, with unbounded delights constantly manifesting themselves, in a journey by the shore of our favorite river, whose name is ever associated with Indian legends, brave deeds and noble sacrifices of daring men and loyal women who made the beautiful Susquehanna Valley to blossom as the rose. And their memories and deeds live on.

Fort Halifax, on the Susquehanna, was contemporary with Forts Hunter, Augusta and other fortifications erected by the English between the years 1740-60. It was ordered to be built in 1756, the work being in charge of Col. William Clapham. The site chosen was on Armstrong creek, which flowed into the river a short distance above the town of Halifax. The creek took its name from three brothers John, Robert and Alexander Armstrong, who located land along its banks and traded with the Indians. Alexander Armstrong was a man of considerable executive ability, as the records show, being entrusted with important business demanding prompt and loyal attention. His brother, John, was the opposite, and a source of trouble and annoyance to him. John early acquired the name of "Captain Jack Armstrong, and he it was who was killed in the celebrated Jack's Narrows on the Juniata, which place took its name from the man and the circumstances therewith related. Of the site of the old fort there is nothing remaining to indicate its position except a spot that is pointed out with no assurance that it is correct. Opposite the town so pleasantly located on the high ground above the river is Clemson's Island, for years the home of the late Leonard Clemson. There are many traditions connected with this island, one of which fixes it as the site of a Shawanese village

Eagle Island, Opposite Halifax.

in 1701. The Indians buried their dead here, the result, it is said, of a bloody battle fought between certain tribes not known. A large mound may still be seen, from which have been taken bones and many relics belonging to the Stone Age.

Gorgas Notch, a high promontory overlooking the river, its perpendicular walls rising two hundred feet above the shore, is on the west bank of the Susquehanna at the great bend above the town of Halifax. The notch is the abrupt termination of Half-Falls mountains and is noted for its weird associations and lonely surroundings. In the steepest side of the rocky ledge, and difficult of approach, one hundred and fifty feet from the tow-path, is the obscure hiding place of the famous outlaw, Simon Girty. For a century it has been known as Girty's Cave and is surrounded with superstitions that grow in gruesomeness and frightful suspicions. There is no path leading to the cave, and one must climb the steep notch to a large rock at the summit, then, with the aid of small saplings, using treacherous rocks for footholds, slowly and carefully descend for a distance of fifty feet, only to be disappointed when the cave is reached. A narrow space permits of two persons standing before the entrance, which is now almost obstructed with the wash and debris from the rocky summit above. There is no doorway, only an irregular opening in the rock, through which one can crawl with difficulty. A small niche above the entrance is called the "window," by means of

which a broad and sweeping view of the river may be had without exposing the body of the watcher. The interior is far from attractive. It consists of but one large room, 37 feet long, 14 feet wide and 9 feet high. The air is very dry and pure, but the general appearance, coupled with the unsavory reputation of the place, renders it disagreeable and repugnant. The cave can be reached only by the circuitous route above described. The tales of Simon Girty's doings in the vicinity of the cave are purely legendary and will not bear close investigation. The elder Girty, also named Simon, was a native of Ireland, and came to America when quite young. He became a trader among the Indians. In 1737 he married Mary Newton, an English girl, with whom he settled down, beginning life at the then notorious locality, Chambers' mill, now Fort Hunter, and some six miles above Harrisburg. Here the younger Simon was born in 1741. He had two brothers, James and George. Chambers' mill was not famous for its morality, and had few rivals for wickedness and general demoralization. The Girty boys early imbibed a love of such company found at the place, and soon excelled in wickedness some of their instruct-

Girty's Cave.

ors. Old man Girty squatted on Sherman's creek, but was ousted by the Sheriff of Lancaster, who burned their cabins and bound the men over to appear for trial at Shippensburg. Subsequently he was killed at Fort Hunter, in a drunken frolic, by an Indian, who, in turn, was shot by John Turner, a friend of Girty's. Two years later Turner married the widow, a woman of unblemished character. Turner, with his wife and stepsons, removed to Sherman's Valley, thence to Fort Granville, now Lewistown, where soon after the fort was captured by a band of French and Indians, the prisoners among whom was Turner and his family were taken to Kittanning, where Turner was burned at the stake in the presence of his wife and her boys. In the years that followed Simon Girty and his brothers took a prominent part in the Indian wars, and stand charged with disloyalty to the colonists during the revolution. Simon was treacherous, bloodthirsty and an enemy of the whites. But once was he known to show mercy to a fellow-being. He became totally blind, and died on his farm, in Canada, not far from Detroit, February 18, 1818. He was buried near the cabin in which he had lived. In 1879 the supposed body of one Albright, the slayer of a man named Miller, which occurrence took place at Montgomery's Ferry, was found in the old cave, it being alleged that the murderer shot himself to avoid the penalty of the law. The body of the supposed murderer and suicide was let down from the mouth of the cave by a long rope. It was discovered by the presence of vultures hovering about the Notch and their attempts to enter the cave. The accompanying illustration is from a photograph, the first ever taken of the famous locality. The river makes a great bend here, turning due south. It is more than a mile wide. The view from the summit of Corty's Notch is wildly grand and fully repays the labor expended in reaching the place of observation.

Millersburg is a popular and enterprising place containing numerous factories and business houses. Wiconisco creek flows into the Susquehanna at the edge of the town. Two brothers, John and Daniel Miller, and Francis Jacques, commonly called "French Jacob," were the first settlers. "French Jacob" built a mill on the creek in 1790, also a large block-

Clump of Trees in Mid River.

house for the protection of settlers, and in which Daniel Miller taught the first school. Millersburg was wonderfully benefited by the discovery of coal in Lykens Valley by Jacob Burd and Peter Kimes in the summer of 1825. The coal was hauled on boats at the mouth of the creek and carried across to Mt Patrick, where it was transferred to boats on the canal. The first boat-load of Lykens Valley coal was shipped in April, 1834, to Thomas Bar bridge at Columbia. Millersburg enjoys a large and lucrative trade with the surrounding country.

Liverpool, on the west bank of the river, is a picturesque town laid out by John Ruggins in 1808. The advantages of the Pennsylvania canal soon made it the most important trading point on the west shore. The passage of the river through the two mountains below renders the scenery exceptionally fine.

Selinsgrove, an old fort town and of considerable importance in the early part of the century, is situated on Penn's creek at its junction with the Susquehanna. In the early settlement of the Penn's creek valley the inhabitants suffered untold atrocities at the hands of the Indians many of whom were Government pensioners. Before the construction of the canal, at the mouth of Middle creek and near where Penn creek empties, there was an island called "The Isle of Q" Charlestown, a suburb, is built on this island. The place was founded by Anthony Sding a German and brother-in-law of the late Gov. Simon Snyder, whose residence was two miles below. Gov. Snyder died in November, 1819, and is buried in the Selinsgrove cemetery. The State, a few years since, erected a monument over his grave. His term of office covered the period between December, 1808, and December, 1817, having been elected three times. During his administration he refused to pardon a certain Philadelphia murderer, whereupon the paramour of the condemned man, a notorious woman, named Ann Smith, alias Carson, with two ruffians left Philadelphia for Selinsgrove for the purpose of abducting the Governor's youngest son and holding him until the pardon was secured. The plot failed, all the conspirators being arrested at Fort Hunter. They were convicted and imprisoned.

THE SONG OF THE WATERS.

I T was midnight on the water
  By fair Susquehanna's shore,
 Floating dimly down the distance
  Came the rapids' sullen roar.
And the campfire's smouldering embers
  Threw a faint and ruddy gleam,
On our tent amid the pine trees
  On the sparkling, moonlit stream.

I was sleepless, and the beauty
  Of the radiant, star-lit night
Drew me down beside the water,
  With an unresisted might.
On the farther shore the mountains
  And the heavens seem to meet
And their deep empurpling shadows
  Stained the current at my feet.

Sweet and faintly sang the waters
  Soft they murmured o'er the stones
And their music seemed to whisper
  In the sweetest, faintest tones.
"I am ancient, very ancient,
  I am aged if a day,
And the centuries, piled on centuries
  Will attest me what I say.

"I could sing of trackless forests
  Never trod by foot of man,
Of the beasts and birds that loved me,
  Through their brief and earthly span.
I could tell of newer ages,
  When the Red man trod the shore,
When the war-whoop's piercing echo
  Rang above the rapid's roar.

"I could sing of Wyalusing
  And her brave Moravian men,
Of the village that they founded
  Far from haunts of mortal ken,
And of Standing Stone, the mighty,
  Close by Wysox's rocky shore
Bronzed and grey with countless ages
  Rich in legendary lore.

PROSE AND POETRY.

"I could tell of war and treachery,
    Of the tomahawk and knife;
Of the tory and the settler,
    And their sharp and bloody strife.
I could sing of fierce Queen Esther,
    And the rock that bears her name;
Of sweet Gertrude of Wyoming
    She of old historic fame.

"I could sing of love and pleasure,
    I could tell of grief and pain,
In the centuries that have flourished,
    That can never come again;
But my duties call me onward,
    I can here no longer bide,
I must haste to lave my ripples
    In the ocean's briny tide."

Then the fretful, babbling current
    Drowned the river's rhythmic tone,
And the water's seemed to murmur
    "I am going, I am gone."
And the moonbeams' silvery halo
    Danced on river, rock and shore,
And again the forest echoed
    To the rapid's sullen roar.

                          WILLIAM MURRAY GRAYDON

December 26, 1885.

SHIKALAMY BLUFF.

SHIKALAMY BLUFF, the high peak on the west side of the river opposite Sunbury, is one of the most noted, picturesque and historic spots on the Susquehanna. Rising to a height of nearly two hundred feet above the river, it is the most prominent landmark between Cæspus Rock and Campbell's Ledge. Its precipitous sides are covered with a scraggy growth of pine and dwarf oaks that take root and scant nourishment among the grey rocks and large boulders.

From the summit of the bluff a panorama of unsurpassed loveliness and wild natural beauty lies before the beholder stretching away to the North, East, and South like an unbroken dream of voluptuous perfection. At its feet is the junction of the West Branch with the main body of the glorious river that

Shikalamy Bluff, Opposite Sunbury.

comes down from the North. The width of the river below the confluence is one mile and is a popular resort for oarsmen and all lovers of aquatic sports. On the summit of the Bluff Shikalamy is a large and commodious hotel, where guests from all parts of the State spend the hot season.

In the early part of the eighteenth century there was great trouble among the several Indian tribes that lived on, or frequented the Susquehanna, whose lovely valley was the favorite hunting grounds of the Iroquois or Six Nations. Chief Shikalamy, after whom the hunt is appropriately named, was elected to preside over the villages on the Susquehanna and Juniata, and came among them in the full vigor of manhood, possessed of nobleness of purpose, humane instincts and intelligent christian character. Shikalamy was of the Cayugas, a powerful tribe, whose principal village was on the present site of Cayuga, in the State of New York. He spent his youth in Canada, where he received instruction, religious and educational, from the Jesuit priests, and was baptized in the Catholic faith. In later years he embraced the creed of the Moravians, in which belief he died in the month of April, 1749. Shikalamy married Nenaoma, a young Indian woman of great beauty and sterling virtues, by whom he had a daughter and three sons; one of the latter being Logan, the Mingo Chief, who made his home for many years in the Kishacokilas Valley. Nenaoma was born at Shamokin and grew to womanhood surrounded by all the wild barbarities and picturesque scenery of her tribe and locality. The coming of the young Cayuga chief, and his subsequent wooing of Nenaoma and their happy marriage, is most charmingly told by that gifted poet Trinam H. Purdy, Esq., a distinguished citizen of Sunbury, and member of the Northumberland bar,—

"SHIKALAMY."

Where Susquehanna's tranquil branches meet,
Like prince and princess, each from far retreat,
And meeting wed, becoming henceforth one,
Was Nature's daughter, Nenaoma, born.

Blue Hill which has for many ages frowned
Upon the less imposing hills around,
Rock-breasted, mountain-walled, had ever been
The legendary home of wondrous men.
Upon its crest of crags a Chieftain stood
And overlooked the river and the wood;
He carried weapons worthy of a man,
But to the past his thoughts of glory ran.
His braves in battle never knew retreat
And yet the world seemed hollow at his feet,
For what were triumphs to a man whose breath
In age began to compromise with death?

From far Cayuga he had brought his son
To see his people where these rivers run,
For these Six Nations, which had been his pride,
His son should rule when he, their chief, had died.
Across the river, where the rippling waves
Press round the Capes as it to kiss their graves,
His noblest warriors, one by one,
Had gone in silence to the setting sun,—
To that imagined "Happy Hunting-Ground;"
Where fadeless youth and endless joys abound.

His son was but the child of woods and waves,
Caressed by winds, and taught by birds and braves;
And he, while gazing from the ledges, spied
A youthful maiden at the river side.
He staid not in his father's thoughts, nor tears,—
His heart and hopes, went out to future years,
And quick descending from the rocks he came
To give his own and ask the maiden's name.
"My father is Oneida's Chief," he said
And "I am Nenaoma," quoth the maid.
They met like children, each admiring, stood
Between the river and the fringe of wood.
He gave her presents carved from tooth of bear,
And wove the partridge-berry in her hair,
And told her tales of Northern lake and glen,
Of fish, of birds, of forest, and of men.
And she, her pleasure and her skill to show
Bound terns and feathers to his polished bow;
She was by nature mistress of those arts
Which work such havoc with untutored hearts.
And with a fairy's step she touched the sand,
Coquetting with her prince from Northern land.

    The old Chief's mission was at last fulfilled,
His government to his son was willed;
But so enticing was this lovely plain
That Shikalamy pleaded to remain.
His mild entreaties were denied and spurned,
And to the North his youthful face was turned,
His feet obeyed; but he in thought was still
With Nenaoma by the Towering Hill.

                *   *   *

    The bright full moon of August came at last,
And o'er Shamokin all its splendors cast;
And where the North and Western Branches meet
Was heard the coming of the festive feet;
A gallant band, a brilliant native train
That ne'er shall grace that shining shore again.
    Young Shikalamy, with his Northern braves,
Came there amidst the old ancestral graves,
And in his native costume, richly dressed,
With belts of wampum, crossed upon his breast,
With head-gear lit by crystals from the mine,
And bracelets wrought from quills of porcupine,
And cloak of ermine fur, he stood to claim
The sweetest bride that e'er to chieftain came.
    Than Nenaoma, none could be more fair,—
Wild roses from the hill-side graced her hair.

And hung in wreaths and festoons lightly round
Her charming form, and trailed upon the ground,
Her eyes shone like the gleaming of a star,—
Her robes were trophies, both of peace and war.

This wedding was unique, and strange to say
Some of the guests have never turned away;
But still remain around these honored dead,—
Around the spot where Shikalamy wed.

Sunbury, the county seat of Northumberland, stands on the site of Fort Augusta, erected by the provincial government in 1756. For years it was the most important military post in Pennsylvania. Many councils between the settlers and Indians were held here. The situation is one of the most desirable along the river. The city stands on a plain bordering the left bank of the Susquehanna river, immediately below the junction of the West and North Branches, and above the mouth of Shamokin creek. It is a thriving place, made so by its proximity to the coal and iron regions, and being the eastern terminus of the Philadelphia and Erie railroad and the junction of it with the Northern Central road. The town proper was laid out and incorporated as a borough in 1797. It has many manufacturing industries and is a delightful place of residence.

Northumberland is situated opposite Sunbury, at the point formed by the confluence of the North and West Branches of the Susquehanna. Its locality is unsurpassed for natural beauty and picturesqueness. The river is spanned by bridges which afford convenient means of travel. The place was laid out in 1775, by Reuben Haines, a Philadelphia brewer, and in infancy was looked upon as one of great promise. Dr. Joseph Priestly, the eminent scientist, lived and died here. He was the discoverer of oxygen gas and the founder of the modern school of chemistry. He was born in England, in 1733, and died at Northumberland in 1804. His grave is marked by a simple monument. In his honor the "Centennial of Chemistry" was celebrated in Northumberland, in August, 1874, many of the most distinguished scientists being in attendance.

FAIR WYOMING.

MATCHLESS vale, when first the white man's eye
Caught a bright glimpse from yonder fissure high,
He saw the ideal of the poet's dream
And claimed thy beauties for the poet's theme.
To him no fairer region had the sun
In his revolving journeys beamed upon:—
Pure, limpid rills, bright skies and balmy air;
Rich flowers, glad promise to the planter's ear,
The painted hills, the checkered beauty proud,
Flecked with the varying shadows of the cloud;
From Lackawanna's gap to Nanticoke,
Crowned with embattled pines and vine-wreathed oak,
The mighty river pours its brimming tide,
While bending o'er the marge on either side,
Scarlet and purple flowers inflame the wood
And on the stream reflect their mantling blood!

Smith's Island.

What wonder that of this romantic vale
To distant lands went forth th' alluring tale?
That blue-eyed Saxon and Mercurial Celt
Came to tiled homes where perfect freedom dwelt?
That bleak New England sent her thrifty men
To seek for richer fields in this fair glen?
That warmed to life by Campbell's tender tale
Of Gertrude, fairest flower of all the vale,
Old Pantisocracy would fain renew
The social fabric which a Plato drew?

The days of settlers' strife and feud are o'er;
Peace spreads her wings on Susquehanna's shore.
If hardy life condemns to daily toil

That rich rewards rise teeming from the soil?
How large the promise made to honest worth
Of a new Eden on this troubled earth?
On Susquehanna's banks, an age of gold,
Like the pure age by ancient poet's told
When man once more, as in his first abode,
Secure from sin and ill might walk with God.

HENRY COPPÉE

1848.

FAIR WYOMING.

"FAIR Wyoming—sweet vale of Wyoming? What innumerable pens have traced thy praises, and what songs the poets have sung of thy lovely landscapes, glorious sunrises and enchanting twilights!" And thy sad history. Oh, Wyoming? Ah, but the years have dried up the springs of sorrow and pathetic memories until one looks back through history's records with but momentary thoughts of horror and vague imagination.

The beauties of the Wyoming Valley were sources of comment by traders, who frequented the North Branch of the Susquehanna, as early as 1692, but were kept from getting hold of land by the Delaware Indians until after the middle of the seventeenth century. The valley lies on the Susquehanna, between Nanticoke on the south and Campbell's Ledge on the north, and is about twenty-two miles long by three miles wide. The valley is surrounded by mountains that rise nearly one thousand feet above the river. From the mighty summit of Campbell's Ledge, looking southward, the lovely valley may be seen in one view, as a

Norfield. Dimes. Eagle's Nest.

charming whole; its lofty mountains forming such well-defined boundaries as to exclude the more distant objects from mingling in the prospect. The valley is one immense industrial hive, where the mechanics, manufacturers, miners and artisans of whatsoever name mingle in daily converse and indulge in social rivalries. The Indians dearly loved the Vale of Wyoming, a name supposed to be a corruption of "Maughwanwame"—the large plains. After repeated proffers for land the Delawares, in 1765, sold the valley to a Connecticut company, who soon brought settlers to occupy the newly acquired territory. Although made in good faith and for an acceptable price, the Indians regretted their action that soon generated a bitter feeling of strife requiring years to quench. The Connecticut people objected to a party of Pennsylvanians who had also located in the valley, and between them a bitter feud arose. The Indians, knowing well the mistake made by disposing of their land to the Connecticut company, and believing the dissensions among the whites would lead to further war in which they, the Indians, could take part and get their revenge, sought many ways to continue the bitter feeling and left no opportunity pass without showing their savage thirst for massacre and extermination. The Delawares alone remained as a tribe when the French war began, the Shawnee's having removed to Ohio and the Nanticokes fearful of proximity to the whites had gone to New York, thus leaving the Delawares in possession of the valley. The latter, after Braddock's defeat, openly declared for the French,

Where the Susquehanna leaves the Wyoming Valley.

and took active part in many of the murderous expeditions on the frontier. This restlessness was for a time quieted by the Philadelphia Quakers and Sir William Johnson, who had built for them houses and loaded them with munificent presents. The quarrel between the settlers from Connecticut and those from Pennsylvania broke out anew and with increased bitterness. The Pennsylvanians represented by Charles Stewart, Amos Ogden and John Jennings secured by stratagem several Connecticut men and placed them in jail. This was the commencement of the civil war which lasted for six years." All efforts at negotiation looking toward a settlement were in vain. Both sides were in alternate possession and forts and block-houses were built, some of which sustained sieges of considerable length. All the expeditions made on either side were more or less failures up until 1775 when the local feuds expired amid the flames of the Revolution. It was a severe and long continued struggle for possession of a prize for which they were willing to contend. The revolutionary war had a beneficial effect upon the Wyoming Valley. The patriotic feeling was intense and the sons of Connecticut and Pennsylvania stood shoulder to shoulder, and finally marched away to join the Continental army. In 1778 Wyoming was an exposed frontier, bordering on the country of the Six Nations, who were numerous, fierce and treacherous. At this time nearly all the able-bodied men were in the American Army and none but aged men, women and children remained behind.

The British had sought the aid of the Six Nations, and planned the desolation of the frontier by the savage horde. The country was also overrun with cowardly tories who sought revenge upon their more patriotic neighbors and assisted the Indians in all their expeditions. Wyoming Valley, in June 1778 was yellow with ripening grain, the barns were partially filled with the earlier crops already housed and the general landscape was

Campbell's Ledge. Where the River Enters the Wyoming Valley.

beautiful in its picture of thrift, contentment and beautiful harvests. But what a terrible fate was in store? On June 30th, a force of four hundred Tories and seven hundred Indians led by Colonel John Butler, entered the valley. The settlers had mustered three hundred men under a brave American, Colonel Zebulon Butler. For a day or two there were frequent skirmishes, the settlers taking refuge in Forty Fort. In the first encounter the settlers lost two hundred men and were almost driven to Wilkesbarre Fort. The slaughter was terrible. Here it was that the half-breed Indian woman, "Queen Esther" tomahawked fourteen wounded settlers in revenge for a son killed in the engagement. After a siege of two days, the inmates on the morning of the fourth surrendered under the promise of being protected by the Indians. No sooner were the gates of the fort thrown open than the slaughter began. The men were nearly all killed, while the women and children were either tomahawked on the spot or held for a more dastardly and cruel fate. The sufferings of the few who escaped were terrible, many seeking shelter at Stroudsburg, where there was a small garrison. Again in 1779, less than a year from the time of the first butchery, the Indians entered the valley. The people were few, weak and ill-prepared for defense, but they concentrated their numbers and made a showing that deterred the savages from further hostilities. After destroying a number of dwellings the Indians left the same way they came. It was during the massacre of July, 1778, that little Francis Slocum, aged five years, and daughter of Jonathan Slocum, was carried away into captivity. Fifty-eight years after she was found in Indiana, the widow of a celebrated Indian chief, to whom she was married, and quite rich in land and stock. The beautiful story of the young captive is graphically told in a recent work by Mr. John F. McGinness, of the West Branch Valley, who gave much time and labor in the securing of facts concerning the pathetic and romantic life of the young woman.

MONTROSE.

PROUD Susquehanna rolls his waters on,
　　Scarce mindful of the changes time has brought;
The Delaware and Iroquois have gone,
　　And every work by nature's children wrought;
Yet the same spirit which her children caught
　From cloud and sunshine, wood and mountain stream,
And which the laws of life and virtue taught
　　Still lingers on the shore, and still the theme
　Inspires of ancient legend and of poet's dream.

Hidden remote in Pennsylvania's hills,
　　Thy vine-clad cottages, O fair Montrose!
Thy fields of green watered by mountain rills,
　　And the pure sparkle of thy winter's snows.
No romance of forgotten years disclose;
　　Yet here strange legends of the past abound.
Here hostile ashes side by side repose,
　　For thine was once the "Dark and Bloody Ground,"
　Where heroes strove for fame, and graves of glory found.

EDWARD A. WARRIMER.

1897.

THE JUNIATA.

—

THE BLUE JUNIATA.

"A Song of Yesterday."

Wild roved an Indian girl,
    Bright Alfarata,
Where sweep the waters
    Of the blue Juniata.
Swift as an antelope
    Through the forest going,
Loose were her jetty locks
    In waving tresses flowing.

Gay was the mountain song
    Of bright Alfarata,
Where sweep the waters
    Of the blue Juniata.
Strong and true my arrows are
    In my painted quiver,
Swift goes my light canoe
    Adown the rapid river.

Bold is my warrior true—
    The love of Alfarata
Proud waves his snowy plume
    Along the Juniata.
Soft and low he speaks to me,
    And then his war-cry sounding,
Rings his voice in thunder loud,
    From height to height resounding.

So sang the Indian girl,
    Bright Alfarata,
Where sweep the waters
    Of the blue Juniata.
Fleeting years have borne away
    The voice of Alfarata,
Still sweeps the river on,
    The blue Juniata.

MRS. MARIAN DIX SULLIVAN.

TWO SONGS.

HE music lore of Pennsylvania is rich in many sweet songs, whose notes and inspiring words cling to one's memory all along the rough and rugged life that leads up to the journey's end. Nor do they fade away as heads grow silvered and bowed with the weight of years, but rather increase in loving favoritism and charming gratification as they are recalled by associations or backward look into the filmy past. But old age cannot dim the voluptuous rhythm of the waltz-like measure, the sentimental sentence so expressive of admiration and love, nor the heaven-created melody that even angels, in their aerial flight, are compelled to look earthward to listen and rejoice.

Old songs! old hymns! old faces!—God bless all of them!

Less than forty years ago that most popular of homely songs, "The Blue Juniata," was known to and sung by everyone, from lisping child to gray-haired parent. It was published far and wide, and the simple melody was heard in cabin or cottage, or wherever the footsteps of a Pennsylvanian wandered in quest of pleasure or fortune. There is in its composition touching memories of the Indian who once roamed the valley of the Juniata, and vivid recollections of other forms and faces and dew-kissed lips that have sung of "Sweet Alfarata," long, ever so long ago. The song was written by Mrs. Marian Dix Sullivan, wife of John W. Sullivan, of Boston, Mass., a son of General Sullivan, of Revolutionary fame. She was a daughter of Timothy Dix, sister of General John A. Dix and Miss Dorothea L. Dix, the great philanthropist, who did so much for sick and wounded soldiers during the war of the rebellion. Mrs. Sullivan was born in Boscawen, N. H., near the beautiful Merrimac river, and died in 1860. It is said the song was inspired by a trip along the Juniata by packet boat before the completion of the railroad between Harrisburg and the Alleghenies.

The "Response to the Blue Juniata" was written in 1865 by Rev. Cyrus Cort, D. D., formerly of Greencastle, Pa., who was then missionary pastor of the First Reformed Church, which he had organized two and a-half years before in Altoona. In the work of raising funds wherewith to erect the present edifice of that congregation, the author preacher had to make frequent trips along the Juniata and its main branches.

It was in the month of August that the spirited little ballad was conceived and woven into rhyme, the author jotting down his poetic inspirations while riding in the cars along this peerless river. In the following month, September, 1865, while traveling with Rev. Dr. H. Harbaugh from Chambersburg to Mercersburg in the favored seclusion of the distinguished divine's carriage, the author showed the poem, which immediately called forth expressions of delight and pleasure and a desire to publish it in his magazine, "The Guardian," which was accordingly done in March following, after much hesitation and consultation with friends. Since then Dr. Cort has written many beautiful things, comprising hymns, poems, odes and the "Bonquet and Brown Memorial."

RESPONSE TO "THE BLUE JUNIATA"

THE Indian girl has ceased to rove
 Along the winding river,
The warrior brave that won her love,
 Is gone, with bow and quiver.

The valley rears another race,
 Where flows the Juniata,
There maidens rove, with paler face
 Than that of Alfarata.

Where pine trees moan her requiem wail,
 And blue waves, too, are kindling,
Through mountain gorge and fertile vale,
 A louder note is swelling.

A hundred years have rolled around,
 The red man has departed,
The hills give back a wilder sound
 Than warrior's whoop e'er started,

With piercing neigh the iron steed
 Now sweeps along the waters,
And bears, with more than wild-deer speed,
 The white man's sons and daughters.

The products, too, of every clime
 Are borne along the river,
Where roved the brave, in olden time,
 With naught but bow and quiver.

And swifter than the arrow's flight,
 From trusty bow and quiver,
The messages of love and light
 Now speed along the river.

The engine and the telegraph
 Have wrought some wondrous changes,
Since rang the Indian maiden's laugh
 Among the mountain ranges

'Tis grand to see what art hath done,
 The world is surely wiser,
What triumphs white man's skill hath won
 With steam, the civilizer

SUSQUEHANNA AND JUNIATA RIVERS.

But still, methinks, I'd rather hear
    The song of Alfarata—
Had rather chase the fallow deer
    Along the Juniata.

For fondly now my heart esteems
    This Indian song and story;
Yea, grander far old nature seems,
    Than art in all its glory.

Roll on, thou classic Keystone stream,
    Thou peerless little river;
Fulfill the poet's brightest dream,
    And be a joy forever.

As generations come and go,
    Each one their part repeating,
Thy waters keep their constant flow,
    Still down to ocean fleeting.

And while thy blue waves seek the sea,
    Thou lovely Juniata,
Surpassing sweet thy name shall be,
    For sake of Alfarata.

REV. CYRUS CORT

JUNIATA

JUNIATA, a word as familiar to every Pennsylvanian as one's own name, and when spoken its meaning and general significance are instantly divined. There is more than ordinary interest attached to it beyond even its historic and romantic associations. Like its sister valley, Wyoming, it was held in almost veneration, which though it might have been by the Iroquois tribes who had villages all along its flowery banks and amid woods and where they hunted and indeed warred with their foes or wooed the dark-eyed Alfarata throughout the unknown centuries. It was their ideal hunting grounds through which ran the endless trail that touched the Susquehanna on the east and the Mississippi on the west, and over which the last Indian passed as fate decreed and the persistent white man forced him so to do. Through all the unwritten lore of the tribes that once claimed the valley of the Juniata as their own, absolute and indisputable, there comes the

"Where the River Mist." Looking Up from Downstream.

echo of regret at surrendering and parting with the lands by the blue Juniata. It is told of a delegation of Indians from Illinois who in 1835 were on their way to Washington, made a special request that they be permitted to pass through the Juniata Valley, the home and hunting grounds of their fathers. The party made the trip by canal boat, which mode of travel afforded every advantage for observation. It is also told that from the time they took passage at Hollidaysburg until Harrisburg was reached there was absolute silence, not a word or gesture to indicate the state of their feelings.

The river "Choniady," as the natives were wont to call it, rises in the Allegheny mountains near Altoona, is joined at Petersburg, seven miles west of Huntingdon, by the Frankstown branch, and, flowing in an easterly direction, empties into the Susquehanna at Duncannon. Its total length is about one hundred and forty-five miles. Its entire course is tortuous, winding in and out of valleys, breaking through mountain ranges and precipitous hills, waters fertile meadows, and has, through nearly its whole course, some of the most grand and picturesque scenery of the State.

Travelers over the Pennsylvania railroad obtain the last view of the Susquehanna as they speed around the bend above the Duncannon station and pass Juniata bridge. The latter was formerly known as "Baskinville," from the original settler who located opposite the confluence of the two rivers. The grand parents of the late Hon. Alexander H. Stephens, of Georgia, were born and raised here.

Club House at Lyndon.

There is a story told that young Stephens and Miss Baskin, when their attachment became apparent to the young woman's parents, made a mutual and solemn vow to be true to each other and be content to "bide awee," hoping that the parental objections might finally become eliminated, or withdrawn. Meantime the French and Indian war came on, and Stephens marched away with Braddock's army. After the war the young colonel, for he had won fame and honor, returned to the mouth of the Juniata to see his affianced. The Baskins still objected to the union, and the loving couple, nothing daunted, resolved to "skip," and brave the parental storm at some future day. They were both willing and the elopement was a mutual success. They left home on horseback, traveled westward and finally settled in Kentucky, where a son, the father of the great Southern orator, was born, but removed to Georgia, the birthplace of his distinguished son.

You have caught the last glimpse of the big river and are fairly launched on a journey unexcelled in variety and beauty of landscape. You pass the Aqueduct, where the Juniata canal joins with that coming down the Susquehanna, also Losh's Run, a choice camping place, with excellent fishing and hunting in the neighborhood, and an old graveyard, where lie the bodies of Marcus Hulings and wife, the first settlers at the mouth of the Juniata on Duncan's Island, although the original homestead is said to be the old tavern above the "Cut" and opposite Aqueduct station. Between the numerous mountain ranges and succession of hills that everywhere greet the eye, a rich and thrifty farm comes into view, a latter-day evidence of the patient industry and frugal lives of the descendants of the first settlers — Irish and Scotch Presbyterians and Germans, the last named coming into the valley after the former had routed the Indians and made life safe and existence free from savage mob station. As early as 1745 the Scotch-Irish explored the Juniata as far west as Standing Stone, now Huntingdon, and doubtless with the intention of locating land as soon as it would be considered judicious and safe. They were the brave and fearless frontiersmen who believed the land was for other purposes than that of hunting, an opinion that determined their actions in the border warfare that followed, carrying with it a hard-earned victory and assurance of future prosperity.

PICTURESQUE IROQUOIS.

Iroquois.

The brakeman thus relieved, fastens back the door with a bang, swings himself to the steps, then to the ground, where he gallantly extends his hand to help you down. Before you have time to ask a question the conductor signals, the bell rings, there is a succession of spasmodic rasping coughs and the steam monster rolls away with its load of humanity and is soon lost to view.

Iroquois! With what familiarity the word impresses one, recalling something from the past of which we have no personal recollection, fostered only by memories of oft-told tales in which romance and realism, preserved by tradition and history, figure so conspicuously. Now that the train is gone and the first sensations one experiences when suddenly transported into a new world have swept across your mental lyre and you feel yourself again, take a glance around and endeavor to find out if you have a fixed habitation within shouting distance, or if the rest of the world can be reached by telephone. For you are in the midst of a mountainous region—there are mountains all around, a canal at your feet and a river within throwing distance. You are in the wilds of Perry county, and among the few signs of civilization are the four endless threads of steel tracks glistening in the sunlight, the dazzling reflections relieved by the gray stone ballast and weather-beaten ties. There is a solitary stone house, built ever so long ago, with background of rocks and trees the abrupt termination of Limestone Ridge, or, as locally known, the Buffalo Hills that has apparently topped short to permit railroad, canal and river to

Iroquois Club House.

pass with lingering echo of whistle, horn and ripple. This is Iroquois, formerly "Poorman's Spring," sometimes called "Half Falls Spring," and twenty-two miles west of Harrisburg, on the line of the Pennsylvania railroad.

The platform on which you stand, in expectation of what may next follow, is elevated about ten feet, and just as you are about descending the steps leading to the footbridge crossing the canal, you are met by a committee from the popular Fishing Club whose guest for the day you must, and very willingly, consider yourself.

"Welcome to Iroquois!" says a well-known Harrisburg gentleman, whose hearty grasp of hand is indicative of the generous disposition of the man. "Glad to see you!" comes in a chorus from a half dozen others; while the baritone voice of a big, fat and jolly coal merchant from the Capital City belches forth, "Aw! stop puttin on airs. Bring him over till we see how he walks the plank." Informal introductions are in order, and a great deal of courteous oratory is dispensed with accustomed liberality. Circumstances peculiar to the place force a compliance with the spirited and imperative request, "to make yourself at home," and you become surprisingly obedient. And being at home, you look around. The club house stands within a few feet of the canal and about thirty yards from the river shore. It is built upon a stone foundation, thus elevating the first floor some twenty feet above low water mark, and on a level with the tow path. The main structure is square, two stories high, with east and west wings. The first story is made of logs, chunked and daubed, the interior being plastered, painted and tastily decorated. The surroundings are neat, cozy and conveniently arranged, while the second floor is used exclusively for more positive rest and recuperation. The kitchen is supplied with a complete cooking pharaphernalia, from spoon to stove, and is where the members display varied and conspicuous skill and originality in the preparation of dainties and substantials for the assembled epicurians. Most men have, at some time, imagined they were chefs, dangerous rivals of the French species—have thought so, and said as much. For that reason the kitchen at Iroquois has witnessed some humorous attempts at following rules laid down in culinary text-books. But there are dishes of Iroquoisian exclusiveness that have a fame extending from the Monongahela to the Delaware, and of which prominent personages—statesmen, politicians, men of the cloth, the brief and scalpel—have partaken and gone away satisfied and possessed of eulogistic enthusiasm. Among the memories that linger around these festal recollections are the Seiler terrapin, the Bergner brew, the Zeigler '68, the Owen punch, the Markley and Bachman planked shad, and many other equally palatable solid and liquid favorites.

When the Harrisburgers, who are sole owners of the place, sought for some secluded spot where they might erect a lodge and woo the sylvan Gods, they wisely secured the old homestead at Poorman's Spring, the tract comprising about sixty acres of timber and cleared land. The charming spring was the real object, the possession of which was the prime inducement leading to the purchase. A man named Poorman is said to have settled in the vicinity in the early part of the present century and christened the natural fountain giving it his own name that has come down through generations to be discarded by the powers that create railway nomenclatures and obliterate traces of the dingy past. With the disappearance of old faces, old customs, habits and pioneer families that made the valley famous in peace or war, also disappeared and going faster year by year, are the still older names of places and localities known the State over. The Iroquois of today was a popular stopping place for wagoners east of the Alleghenies far back into the beginning of the settlement of the Juniata Valley. These men made quarterly trips to and from Philadelphia over the old Pittsburg turnpike, that skirts the opposite shore of the river like a thread leading into the shadowy years of the bygone. The stage coach, with its load of freight and passengers, stopped at the Steckly homestead, where a change of horses was made. In the evening the travelers would indulge in a sport with the oars, crossing to the opposite shore to drink from the old spring. But what memories a talk of those old stage coach days brings forward! Why,—

"We hear no more the clanking hoof and the stage coach rattling by,
For the steam king rules the traveled world, and the pike is left to die.
The grass creeps over the flinty path, and the stealthy daisies steal
Where once the stage horse, day by day, lifted his iron heel.
No more the weary stager dreads the toil of the coming morn,
No more the bustling landlord runs at sound of echoing horn,

For the dust lies still upon the road, and bright-eyed children play
Where once the clattering hoof and wheel rattled along the way.
The coach stands rusting in the yard, the horse has sought the plough;
We've spanned the world with an iron rail, and the steam king rules us now.
The old turnpike is a pike no more—wide open stands the gate;
We've made a road for our horse to stride, which we ride at a flying rate.
On, on, on, with a haughty front, a puff, a shriek and a bound;
While the tardy echoes wake too late to babble back the sound."

But there must have been some peculiar attraction in the refreshing waters that could induce hunter or trapper, or traveler on horseback and stage to cross ostensibly to renew youth and presumably discuss the nature of the backwoods country. Still longer back in the dim past bright Alfarata has roved by these same flower-tipped banks and coquetted with

View From the East Stoop.

her warriors bold, or paddled her light canoe up and down and across the rippling stream. Who knows but this charming Indian woman did not have her trysting-place by the old spring, where she tortured her lovers in a manner that the fair maidens of to-day follow with historical accuracy. Though the story of Alfarata may carry with it a great deal of poetical and romantic imagery, yet there is a fanciful fascination about it that compels one to accept it as a fact.

Should the day be typical of summer or early autumn, your visit to Iroquois will be one of unbroken pleasantries, social chit-chat and enjoyable communings with nature. And long years after you may draw upon imagination and live over again the entertaining moments the memories of which constantly break in upon daily life, adding sweetest fragrance to occurrences gone by. On the broad and shady porch one may sit and look and look at the beautiful panorama of broken landscape. Right below is the river—the blue Juniata—and you instinctively hum a bar or two of that pretty song that Marian Dix Sullivan wrote in her girlhood days, and picture, if you can, the heroine, Sweet Alfarata.

The river is a quarter mile wide, the current disturbed here and there by rifts of sandstone rocks that look out from the surface at the clear sky above. One can hear the incessant musical murmur of the Falls, the echoes wandering back and passing away until lost in the wooded glens. A picture of magnificent grandeur and natural loveliness lies before you. Rough mountain roads, picturesque in their surroundings, forming the most beautiful drives through charming woodland scenery, lead down to, or along the river that flows onward, hemmed in between the Buffalo Hills on the right bank and the three bold headlands of Half Falls mountain on the left. The gap of the Juniata, at Iroquois, is reputed to be the most gorgeous piece of near scenery in many miles. In this instance it is not distance that lends enchantment, but singular and varied beauty that charms. The fishing here is excellent, the owners of the Fish-house stocking the river, from time to time, with small fry and looking after the enforcement of the laws with that zealous spirit inherent in every true sportsman.

"Over! Over!"

Under the weird spell that comes upon one while contemplating the wild and rugged beauties of Iroquois, you have lapsed into a dreamy, half-waking mood, out of which you are aroused by the voice of somebody calling. All around is quietness and the cause of the disturbance is a mystery. Looking up stream in the vicinity of the boat-house, a man woman and two children are seen standing by the big rock that marks the landing for boats. The woman and little folks sit down upon a wait log, while the man continues to look across the river. Presently he puts both hands to his mouth and again comes the sound:— "Over! Over!" The attention of one of the children is attracted by something on the opposite shore, and dropping the handful of sand, runs to the big rock, climbs up and exclaims:—"There's the Ferry Girl's house!" and claps the tiny hands in joyous satisfaction. Do you see that two-story stone-and-log house on the other side of the river? It stands at the foot of the mountain slope and close by the old Pittsburg pike. From the river—a hundred yards away—a much traveled path leads up to the door. Soon a figure appears in the doorway, and a childish form skips down the path to the rude stone wharf. It is a mite of a girl who has probably run ahead of some older person that intends taking the boat across for the party waiting on the Iroquois shore. For this is a ferry, known far and near, and in that old house by the turnpike lives the ferryman, Reuben Shoaller, his wife and family. But the child waits for no one. A large boat, moored beside the wharf, is quickly unfastened, the girl jumps in, picks up the oars with a familiarity that is surprising; drops into the seat and the boat shoots out into the stream. The craft is now fifty feet from the wharf. The girl turns her head, glances toward the opposite side of the river to get her bearings, then settles down to work. See how she bends to the oars? Deep down she dips them, and then, with the strength of a man and skill of an athlete, she pulls long and hard, releasing the tips of the paddles with that easy, rapid grace one sees among rowing people only. Every stroke of the oars sends the boat dancing over the sudsy waves, coming nearer and nearer with the swiftness and grandeur of the swan. The nearness of the craft does not magnify the figure of the rower, who is even smaller than at first supposed when seen on the further shore. The creaking of the oars in the worn locks grows plainer; the wash of the waves sweeps up beyond the wet line, and the tiny pieces of drift disturbed by the incoming swell from the stream, dive and tumble and bow and nod as if acknowledging the *robe* of a mermaid or latter-day water witch. The boat reaches shallow water, scrapes the sand and stops.

"Ready?" queries the girl, standing erect, heedless of the rocking of the restless boat, a flush on her cheeks the result of her trip just ended. There are no signs of fatigue about her, and with a saucy, independent toss of the head, an innocent smile upon her lips, she directs the man and woman how to be seated to advantage, bids the children to keep still, assuring them that she will take them safely over, gives the boat a quick shove and leaps on board. It takes but a moment to swing the boat into position, then with the confidence and air of an old sailor seizes the paddles and "ises a flash the little "Water Witch," and her passengers are swiftly speeding away from the Iroquois shore. Away goes the boat, feeling the effects of every stroke of the oars, dashes across the ruffled bosom of the East side current, swims the placid waters lying next to the shore, and brings up at the wharf with a precise suddenness that almost throws the occupants off their seats.

That was but a glimpse of the Ferry Girl of Iroquois, or as strangers call her, "the little Water Witch." If dashing simplicity, venturesome disposition, womanly daring and absence of fear are essential to the title of "Water Witch," then little Annie Shealer has been appropriately, though informally christened by the patrons of the ferry and others who frequent the neighborhood on pleasure bent. Her acquaintance is limited to those brought into actual contact, many of whom she has ferried across the Juniata, or acted as messenger when the condition of the commissary at the Fish House demanded prompt replenishing. Yet fickle fame has left unsought this little heroine, without crown but with honor in her own country. The youngest of a large family, the brief years—fifteen all told—of Annie's life, have been spent almost exclusively within the shadow of the log house where she first saw the light. For companions she has none, save the dogs that rove the pine hills and keep jealous watch over her in all her daily wanderings. Born beside the river she imbibed all the fondness for aquatic pleasures and exercises that nature involuntarily provided. The father is one of that class of whilom hunters and fishermen, once so common in the Juniata Valley, but of whom only a few remain to rehearse the tales of woodcraft they so cleverly practised. He added to his income the revenues derived from the ferry, which though small, was of considerable aid to the man, the head of a large family, with broad shoulders to clothe and sound appetites to appease. When the father was absent or otherwise engaged the mother of little Annie was left to care for the ferry and its patrons. There is no record of the girl's first trip across the river. She seems to have been rocked on the bosom of the rippling waves, growing into girlhood between the pebble-lined shores. When seven years old Annie was the cause of the most painful anxiety on the part of strangers and the almost distracted mother. The two were alone, the mother engaged in household duties, paying little attention to the ferry or possible patrons liable to come along. Annie, with a pair of big dogs, was down by the river reveling in sunshine and giving no thought to cares or passing hours. An imaginary castle of flat stones, the walls mortised with pebbles and mussel shells, bent twigs representing Knights on horseback, and crisp brown leaves, gaily-decked chariots—the whole a reflection of thought uppermost in the young mind, and a very good impression left by the perusal of some story book—was the result of a half day's persistent work or play. The dogs slept in the sun their noses thrust deep into the cool sand ready to be suddenly awakened in case of emergency or signal from their young mistress. Two men stood on the opposite shore, close by the Fish House. They waved their hands and called for the ferry boat. The child raised her head, tilted back the little faded sun-bonnet and listened. Again she heard the men raising. Annie understood the signal and decided not to interrupt her mother. She ran to where the boats were anchored, climbed in and took the chain off the post. The dogs wanted to join her but were refused. Too small to sit down, she stood with tiny hands grasping the oars which she wielded with remarkably full sweep. She seemed to remember every act of her father with whom she had so often crossed, and carefully followed the course that, at this day, assures an easier pull. The men saw the boat coming, watched its slow but steady progress, never thinking that a child was in charge. By and by she landed and declining to be expostulated with as well as refusing the oars to one of the men, she ordered them in and ferried them over in safety. Carrying the money received for ferriage to her mother, she proudly and laughingly told of the event and, with a show of contempt, of the "fraidy men who couldn't talk for shaking."

When the flood of '89 deluged the river valley and swept away the savings of a lifetime, the Ferry Girl rendered heroic services to neighbors and strangers that shall ever stand as a storied monument to her name and memory. People living among the hills east of the Juniata, were short of provisions which could only be had at the few stores located on the West bank. Much suffering was known to exist and every day saw the situation growing more serious. Men came to the ferry to talk of the great flood and discuss the future, but every proposition to send for relief across the river was declared hazardous and too dangerous to attempt. Neighbors divided their last pound of flour, and many were left with nothing but a small quantity of meat. The flood had come upon them suddenly and found them unprepared. Annie had listened to their complaint and felt no little anxiety for her own household. Early one morning, the water being somewhat higher than the day previous, the girl startled all by announcing her determination to cross the river and take a train for Newport where provisions could be procured. All she asked was money; she would do the rest. Many objected, but without effect, except to make the child more determined. The father was appealed to, but he said she knew what she was doing and he had confidence in her ability and pluck. She took with her a large basket and leather bag, placing the money given by the neighbors in the latter for safe-keeping. The boat was carefully examined, the strength of the oars tested, a hasty good-bye and the brave girl started for the other side of the river. She hugged the shore for a considerable distance up stream, then took a diagonal course, aiming for a huge oak tree standing a hundred yards above the Iroquois fish house, and landed on the bank of the canal. The tow path was partly under water, but with almost superhuman strength she drew the boat into the canal, reaching the station in time for a train to Newport. Returning in the afternoon she found the water had receded and recrossed the river in safety.

During the summer Annie has the exclusive control of the ferry, crossing the river as often as twenty times in one day. In appearance she is of slender build, erect carriage, quick and graceful step. Her face, childish in form but expressive of great determination, with prominent lines indicating fearlessness and combative force, is crowned by a mass of well-kept dark brown hair, and lighted by a pair of piercing black eyes that scintillate and dance with merriest, but positive and vigorous intimations when their owner wields the paddles. Her hands are small, the forearm thin with no noticeable prominence of muscle. In the remarkable development of the biceps lies the secret of the girl's success and endurance as a rower. A prehensile movement of the arm—a grasp unyielding and firm—displays a mass of hard muscle, extending to, and including the sterno and scapulary coverings, affording a powerful grip and retentive strength that is astonishing. The child has never had a coacher nor the advice and example of one skilled and trained in athletic or aquatic exercises; nor has she ever witnessed a rowing contest. All her work has been done in the old ferry boat, a big, heavy and clumsy boat that severely taxes the strength of strong and able-bodied men. Given a boat of proper size and weight, a shell constructed for fast rowing, and a teacher that understands his art and pupil, there is no risk in asserting that the world might not have long to wait for an opportunity to huzza and laud the champion of the oar in the person of the little Water Witch of Iroquois.

Walk down a gently sloping path leading to the river and you stand on the verge of Iroquois' treasure. The waters laugh and sparkle with the roguishness of a woman's lips and  eyes till one is tempted to hug and kiss the very walls for gratification or revenge. Standing thus by the historic landmark you readily understand and appreciate the popularity the place has always enjoyed. It is a fact, remarkable to many, that there is but one spring of water of nearly equal capacity, between Harrisburg and Newport, other than that at Iroquois. The one referred to is near the town of Marysville, and was dug out and walled by the late D. W. Seiler, then engineer of construction on the Northern Central railway. It is not known who built the original walls at Iroquois, long

The Old Spring.

since gone to ruin. They were rude, of native stone and constructed without regard to design, height or width. The flood of '89 damaged the Club's grounds, the surroundings of the spring being among the general wreck. When repairs were made the spring was enlarged and remodeled. It is shaped like a horse-shoe, is fifteen feet long and ten feet wide. The quantity of water discharged per minute is estimated at one hundred gallons. The fountain head is in Limestone Ridge, just above the railroad, the water finding its way through the strata of rocks that terminate a few feet above the outlet. The water has no known specific medicinal properties and its reputation rests solely and securely on its warranted purity, refreshing and invigorating qualities.

A hundred yards below the spring a long irregular ledge of rocks crosses the river at right angles. These gray, water-washed fragments were, doubtless, once an impregnable barrier to what has since become the natural water course, affording perfect and complete drainage to the Juniata Valley. These rocks form a beautiful cascade or falls of singular charm and impressive effect. They span the entire width of the stream, making a dam fully ten feet deep at any season of the year, driving the water back to a level that reaches Bailey's more than a mile above. In summer the scene is ravishingly picturesque, the wild surroundings being increased in weird magnificence by mountains and wooded hills whose feet are washed by the murmuring waters. Iroquois Falls attracted the attention of the engineers who constructed the canal, they deeming it wonderfully advantageous as a dam from which to feed the proposed canal. It was at one time under serious consideration, and only the magnitude and cost of the undertaking, the limited finances and the risk supposed to attend it, prevented the consummation of the project. When the flat boat and ark were seen upon our inland streams, and the means of transportation were limited to the wagon, the pack horse and river boat, the navigation of the Juniata was one of the heroic sides to the life of the pioneer. To get over the Iroquois Falls was an effort requiring strength of muscle, tact, patience and pluck. Whole days, it is told, were consumed hauling the boats over the treacherous rocks; while often they were relieved of their freight and the empty boat dragged on shore and thence around the falls. In one or two of the larger rocks the iron staples yet remain to tell of these struggles for civilization.

On a point of land, barren and desolate, just below the rocks, is the old burying-ground —so old that local traditions have no positive record of its first use for interment of the dead. It is a secluded and lonely spot, the ground sloping toward the shore and partially hidden within the shadows of large old oaks that stand like faithful guardians over the slumbering dead. Who they were, or what they did, is unknown so far as careful inquiry could discover. A few rude stones mark the dimensions of the graves. On one is carved in large figures, "1808," the only inscription, but meaningless as to identity of the dead. On another, but almost effaced, are the initials, "C. G." Old settlers have told that the place was the favorite Indian burying-ground, and the land lying between the river and where the canal now is was once covered with headstones and mounds, beneath which were dead Indians numbering many scores. No attempt was ever made to excavate for relics of the departed, that the legends might be verified or proven mythical. There are seven distinct mounds, with head and foot stones in position, but residents of the neighborhood assert that they well recollect when the sacred limits included all the hillock referred to. This land was once owned by the Hulings and Watts families. There is no doubt but the Iroquois graveyard contains the bones of departed pioneers from Sherman's, the Tuscarora and Buck's Valleys, whose descendants are ignorant of their resting place. Tradition has it that in 1780 a small log church was erected by the few Lutherans living near the spring. It was, according to the same authority, burned down in 1804. The remains of what was once a foundation wall may still be seen above the old burying-ground.

The locality was not only famous for its spring and burial ground, but because of its being the natural outlet, or short cut between the two rivers. One of the oldest known Indian trails, and one which the white settlers followed in traveling from Northeastern Pennsylvania to beyond the Alleghenies, crossed the Susquehanna at Montgomery's Ferry, led through Buck's Valley to Iroquois, known at that date as "Half Falls," thence west through the Juniata Valley. Settlers from all the valleys bordering on the Juniata river tramped over the same path to and from Wilkesbarre and the Northeast, considering it a great saving of time and travel as compared with the trail through the Lebanon Valley to Harrisburg and westward along the river. Here the celebrated Shawnee Chief, Shikalamy, whose village was in the vicinity of Sunbury, met the old Chief, Kishecokilas, also of the Shawnee nation, and conferred concerning the constant increase in numbers of white settlers that were taking possession of the fertile valleys crossing the Juniata. Both chiefs were the friends of the settlers, and evidenced their loyalty in every possible way. Kishecokilas was not as powerful and influential as Shikalamy, but could control many of the villages, and the young warriors looked to him for counsel and advice. With Kishecokilas came Logan, whose title, "Mingo Chief," as well as the reputation for fealty to the settlers which he possessed, maintains for him a niche in local history. Logan was the second son of Chief Shikalamy and went into the Juniata Valley presumably as the friend of old Kishocokilas, companion and fellow-warrior of his noted father. Consequently when Kishocokilas received Shikalamy's request for a conference, Iroquois, or Half Falls Spring, was selected as the place. Chief Shikalamy was of the Cayugas, a powerful tribe, whose principal village was situated on Cayuga Lake, in New York. He was deputed to rule the Shawnees, who had been received into the alliance thereafter known as the Six Nations. He had been converted by the missionaries, and when he came among the Shawnees he soon obtained a great influence over them. They were dissolute, blood thirsty and treacherous, but Shikalamy ruled them with kindness, backed by an iron will and indomitable courage. He was strictly temperate, because he was credited with saying, "I never wished to become a fool." The council between the two chiefs lasted for several days, the accompanying Indians indulging in fishing and hunting. The spring was considered by the Indians as sacred, they believing that the Great Spirit drank from the fountain, and the water, in consequence, was blessed and possessed virtues to prolong life and assure freedom from danger and disease.

IROQUOIS.

AWAY from the city's bustle and roar,
    The madd'ning rush of the frigid world;
From the endless grind of the helpless poor,—
    O lives so crushed and ruthless whirled!
To the beautiful river I'll gladly go,
    With reverence worship the Gods of Joy;
Dream of one spot, but one below
    This side of heaven: 'Tis Iroquois.

And there 'neath the shade of primeval trees,
    Charmed by the ripple's lullaby song,
I'll tell my soul to the fragrant breezes—
    A pledge of love both true and strong.
No envy or care shall dare intrude,
    The bitter of life must be forgot;
The Spring, the Falls, the sacred dead
    E'er bless and hallow the lovely spot.

Drift on, O waters of storied blue,
    Nor heed the waves that swell and dip;
Smile but on those who can be true,
    Kiss hill and vale with red-ripe lip.
Flow on, O Juniata, fair,
    With gentlest murmur and softest sigh;
Far though I wander, far from here,
    I'll never, never, say "Good-bye."

                                        ZENAS J. GRAY.

UP THE RIVER.

BAILEY'S is an old-time packet-boat station and the location of "Old Caroline Furnace," one of the earliest of its kind east of Millerstown. The place took its name from the owner, Hon. Joseph Bailey, a gentleman of the old school, member of Congress and manufacturer. The land here was first settled by the Van Camps in 1762. They came originally from Holland, settling at Kingston, New York, which place they left hastily in terror of Indian Massacre, bringing away with them all their effects on the backs of horses. The ruins of the old furnace together with a few of the tenement houses are still standing. There is a legend that in the Buffalo Hills lying between Bailey's and Iroquois the Indians got their supply of lead but refused to indicate to the whites the location of the mines.

The river has numerous curves, short and sharp, the railroad swinging around Trimmer's Rock and along the base of the mountain until Newport is reached. The town was

Trimmer's Rock, East of Newport.

laid out by Daniel Reider in 1814 and took the name of "Reider-ville." The building of the canal in 1830 brought a prosperous trade and it was called "New Port." It was the gateway to the rich valleys of Perry county, an immense trade being transacted for more than sixty years. A narrow gauge road built as far west as New Germantown, connects here with the Pennsylvania road. While making the canal a large stone shaped like a Greek cross was dug up on the site of the Indian town just north of the borough limits. On it were cut hieroglyphics and data that mystified the residents as to its origin and history. Careful research has, however, revealed its story. About 1771 two Jesuit priests came from Canada with

the design of founding a mission among the Juniata Indians, reaching the valley near the site of Newport. The priests cut the cross out of native sandstone and which formed part of their rude altar. Failing in their object to build a church the cross was buried and the Jesuits with the Indians, went toward the setting sun.

Millerstown is on the east bank of the river, one mile above the dam so familiar to boatmen and anglers. It is a beautiful sheet of water across which canal boats are towed with an endless rope, being operated by water power. Indulging in a geological talk which is appropriate at this time, Professor Claypole says very few people have any idea of the amount of work done by a single river like the Juniata in transporting the land from adjacent hills into the sea. In ordinary weather a gallon of Juniata water carries about eight grains of earthy sediment or one pound for every one hundred cubic feet. At the

Millerstown dam the river is six hundred feet wide and four feet deep, with a current flowing two miles an hour; that is 21,000,000 cubic feet of water pass over the dam every hour, carrying 210,000 pounds (120 tons) of rock sediment. In other words, 1,000,000 cubic yards of rock waste of Juniata, Mifflin, Huntingdon and Blair counties pass down the Juniata river to the sea every year. The water basin from which this river sediment comes measures about 10,000,000,000 square yards. Its average loss per year is, therefore, about the ten thousandth of a yard, and counting the gravel and stones carried down in flood times and by ice, it will be safe to call it the five thousandth of a yard. Thus the whole surface of the Juniata Valley has been lowered say one foot in 1500 years, or 3,000 yards in 13,500,000 years.

A few miles east of Millerstown, in Pfoutz's Valley, is old St. Michael's Lutheran church. The congregation was organized in 1760, worshiping in private cabins and later in the old log school-house built on the graveyard plot. The first church was erected in 1798, a new one taking its place in 1847. The early settlers, many of whom were murdered by the Indians, lie buried here.

Thompsontown, on the left bank, and one mile from the railway station which is reached by a high bridge across the Juniata, is quite an old town, with a prosperous country inside. Mexico is a wayside station and is prominent in local history as the locality settled by an ambitious Scotch-Irishman, Captain James Patterson, who came across from Cumberland county in 1751. He was accompanied by others who located in the vicinity. Two large log houses were quickly built, the sides being pierced with loopholes in readiness for an Indian attack which they expected. In locating at Mexico, Patterson defied the proprietors whom he did not consult and would not purchase from the Indians with whom he had frequent encounters with rifle and knife. They called him "Big Shot," on account of his expertness with the rifle. Later he was forced to leave and seek shelter in Sherman's Valley, but returned to find that the Penn's had parcelled out his land and it was occupied by strangers. He secured another tract and again refused to pay for it, holding that if it was right for the Penns to cheat the Indians out of millions of acres of land it was no wrong in him to cheat the Penns out of a farm. In the war upon the whites commencing in 1763, the Tuscarora settlements suffered the most horrible massacres, many of their children being carried beyond the Ohio.

Port Royal is on the west bank of the river, at the end of the "Tuscarora Path Valley," extending from the Gap at Concord, to the Juniata river. A narrow gauge railroad has just been completed, which will aid in making the place one of business importance.

Mifflintown, the county-seat of Juniata county, is delightfully situated on the left bank of the river, opposite the railway station, which latter place also takes the same name, being formerly known as Patterson. The town occupies a sloping eminence, from which a view of the surrounding scenery is afforded. An open iron bridge connects the two portions of the town. The repair shops of the Pennsylvania railroad were located here prior to their removal to Altoona. Bell's Island is a fertile tract on which one of the many mythical "Grasshopper Wars" is said to have taken place between two tribes of Indians. The town was founded in 1791 by John Harris, a native of County Donegal, Ireland, and not by John Harris, of Harris' Ferry, who was an Englishman. The similarity in names has doubtless led to such confusion in the Colonial Records, all credit being given the Harris of Paxtang. The Mifflintown Harris was also prominent in his day and it is a matter of sincere regret that so little authentic history of the man and his time has been preserved. In the pretty cemetery there are four massive marble slabs with the inscriptions less satisfactory than the meagre traditions that have come down to the present. The first records the death of James Harris, believed to be the brother of John Harris, which occurred September 1, 1804, in his 58th year. Beside James' tomb is that of John Harris, the founder of the town, the inscription being copied in full:—

> "Here lieth the body of
> John Harris, Esq.,
> who departed this life, Feb. 28, 1794,
> Aged about 71 years.

"He was born in the County of Donegal, in Ireland; came to this country in early life. Educated in the principles of religion and morality, he was exemplary in the performance thereof. He possessed a large share of public confidence; in the character of a magistrate he was judicious; as a legislator he was discerning and determined, and in the worst of times showed himself his country's friend and the friend of man. As a husband, a father, a relation or a friend he was beloved, honored, respected and in his death by all lamented."

The third grave is that of his wife, Jean Harris, who died in 1807 aged 83 years. The inscription on the fourth and last slab says that William Harris, presumably the son of John and Jean, died in 1807 in his 18th year. Mifflintown possesses many fine homes, the residents being enterprising and thrifty. The surrounding country is well-cultivated and highly productive. The elevation is 151 feet above tidewater.

A ride of four or five miles along the Juniata and the train enters the celebrated Lewistown Narrows, the wildest and most beautiful scenery which the eye of the tourist could

Lewistown Narrows.

desire. The Black Log mountain is on the right bank of the river, while the Shade mountain guards the left. Looking out of the car window and upwards you see, perched upon the very summit of both mountains, huge, rocky promontories black and dismal, and broken in irregular heaps of detached rocks held in place by some small sapling or deepest rock. Covered with moss and of a dark and sombrous color, they give to the scene a stamp of positive wildness, the beauty of which is increased by the overhanging foliage, sloping to the rugged banks of the Juniata, which leaps over its rocky bed as if bewildered by the scene around. There are many other scenes in our mountain ranges similar to this; but there is none in this blessed continent which surpasses it in picturesque outline. It is one of those things, too, that must be seen leisurely to be fully comprehended and enjoyed. Rushing through this mighty gorge one can but feel as though passing through a land of strange and weird scenes, interspersed by gleams of sunshine and music of splashing waterfall. A ride through the "Long Narrows" is a pleasure never forgotten nor regretted.

Rolling up the gentle, but perceptible, grade of fifty-seven feet in twelve miles, Lewistown is reached, west from Harrisburg sixty-one miles; from Philadelphia, one hundred and sixty-two miles. Arthur Buchanan, also a Scotch-Irishman, from the Cumberland Valley, took up land where Lewistown now stands and built the first cabin in 1755. About the same time Fort Granville was erected a mile above. The site of the fort has long since disappeared. The Indians butchered the inmates in the summer of 1756, after a brave and desperate resistance. Near Lewistown is the famous Kishocokilas Valley, the home of Chief Kishocokilas, the friend of Shikalamy at Shamokin, and with whom the latter's son, Logan, the Mingo Chief, lived and hunted for many years. Lew-istown was laid out in 1790 by James Potter and William Brown. The place is noted for its fine scenery, railway and manufacturing facilities, and all the desired advantages of a prosperous inland city. Eleven miles above is McVeytown, an old established fort village and formerly of considerable importance. Near it is Hanawalt's Cave, from which the Indians obtained saltpeter used by them in making powder and the curing of venison. Ryde is a bewildering little place of a dozen houses, grist-mill and cemetery. A half-mile above and close by the river bank stands the pretty resort of the Altoona Hunting and Fishing Club. A charming bit of sandy beach stretches along the premises, reminding one of seaside spots haunted by mermaids and water witches.

Club House at Ryde

Newton Hamilton, noted for its Methodist Camp Grounds, has, since the abandonment of the canal, lost much of its prestige. West of here the river makes a sharp bend, over which the railroad crosses on a bridge seventy feet above the water.

Mount Union, with an altitude of five hundred and ninety feet above ocean tide, is built at the entrance to the old Aughwick Valley, so renowned in the early settlement of the Juniata. It has numerous iron manufactories, extensive tanneries and a large trade with the valleys that open toward the river. It is the junction of the East Broad Top road that now runs through the Shade Gap and into the ore fields in Shade Valley. In the vicinity are rich mines of iron ore used for home consumption and foreign shipment.

Leaving Mount Union, the railroad, without observing the formality of an introduction, rushes the traveler into the world-famous "Jack's Narrows," in the very midst of mountains that are bold, rugged and far beyond description. The name, "Jack's Narrows," or "Jack's

Mountains' were so called from the fact that one, John Armstrong whose home was on Armstrong's creek, in Dauphin county, now Halifax, with two hired men, James Smith and Woodward Arnold were killed by an Indian Musemelin. The murder was committed in February, 1744 and created a great deal of talk among the Indians at Sunbury and the white settlers on the Susquehanna. "Jack" Armstrong was given to drink, and was possessed of few principles that make up the man. He had dealings with the Indian Musemelin from whom he took a horse as security for a debt that mysteriously grew larger, though the Indian made frequent payments. Armstrong and his servants went to the Narrows to trade and there meeting Musemelin, the latter demanded his horse. Armstrong refused, and the Indian determined upon revenge. Following Armstrong's party, he succeeded in killing all three and buried their bodies among the rocks. The place of sepulture is said to be on the summit of Rocky Ridge, west of Mapleton, where, it is alleged, remains of a human body were discovered in 1888. Near Mapleton, in 1789, Samuel Drake

Tiew in Jack's Narrows.

established a ferry, which, for fifty years, was the great crossing-place over the Juniata. Another individual, called "Captain Jack," "The Black Hunter," etc. and a veritable hater of Indians haunted the Narrows after the murder of Jack Armstrong. The "Black Hunter" settled in Aughwick Valley, removing to the Narrows in 1755, where his exploits and the terrible vengeance he inflicted upon the Indians soon made him friends among the frontiersmen. He led a company of scouts, or rangers and offered his service to General Braddock, who refused them on account of Jack's unwillingness to be enrolled as a regular company. The "Black Hunter" is said to have died in 1772.

Huntingdon, ninety-seven miles west of Harrisburg, is the county seat of Huntingdon county. It was laid out at the mouth of Standing Stone creek, in 1770, by Dr. Smith, the then Provost of the University of Pennsylvania, in honor of Selina, Countess of Huntingdon, a liberal contributor to the funds of that institution. Prior to this time the place was known as "Standing Stone," the Indians having a village there. A fort was erected in 1762 for the better protection of the frontier. It has long since been noted for its beautiful location on the left bank of the Juniata the wealth and intelligence of its citizens and the enterprise and success of its business ventures. Furnaces, for smelting lead and iron ore, were erected as early as 1792 its mineral wealth having but few rivals. At Petersburg, seven miles west of Huntingdon the Frankstown branch joins the Juniata which dwindles gradually into a small mountain brook, whose source is high up in the Allegheny mountains.

JACK'S NARROWS.

ALL hail thou deep and mighty gorge,
    That mak'st for man the way;
Thou wondrous work of nature's hand,
    On old creation's day,
With awe I view thy rugged slopes,
    And mark thy tow'ring heights,
Where mountain grandeur clothes each view
    With wild and lovely sights.

Dell's Ferry.

And proud thou art that at thy feet
    As peaceful measures glide,
The Juniata's limpid waves
    Thy rocky steeps divide.
And mirror from their placid depths
    Thy pines and oaks so old,
Whose mossy trunks and moss-clad boughs
    Heed not the heat or cold.

Upon the gray and hoary cliffs
    That crown thy winding way,
That stand like castles, old and grim,
    Untouched by rude decay.

The eagles rear their helpless young
    From all their foes secure,
And teach their timid wings to range
    To ether clear and pure.

When vernal skies dispel the chill
    That winter winds have brought,
And heal the wounds with piteous hands
    Unfeeling frost hath wrought;
Then woodland beauty hastens forth
    Thy bleak defiles to hide,
And leaflets spring from tree and shrub
    And flowers on every side.

If summer suns, with melting ray,
    Make hills and valleys glow,
And fling their beaming radiance down
    Alike on friend and foe;
With gentle breezes then art fanned,
    With balmy zephyrs blest,
Refreshing to the languid ones,
    And to the weary rest.

So, too, when autumn's mellow days
    Begin their busy hours,
And hang their gorgeous drapings wide
    O'er all thy sylvan bowers,
Then many a low and laden bough
    And many a stately tree,
With gen'rous yield their fruits bestow
    A bounty rich and free.

But they have left thy wooded wastes
    And sought an unknown strand;
Their fires are out, their wigwams gone
    To rise in spirit-land;
They tread no more thy mazy paths,
    Nor cross thy rocky bounds
But tread in blissful ecstacies
    Their happy hunting grounds.

And then a race superior came
    To wake thy sleeping scenes,
To hew a passage through thy length
    And bridge thy dark ravines;
Their beasts of burden came and went
    Their wide and beaten way,
While great and lumbering wagons passed
    In haste both night and day

SUSQUEHANNA AND JUNIATA RIVERS.

They smoothed still more the broad highway
  With most untiring skill
And sent the daring stage-coach
  To speed along at will.
And when the echoing horn rang out,
  In din both wild and new,
Thine Alpine peaks and deep retreats
  Soon faded from the view.

But when the storms of winter come
  Thy solitudes to claim,
Old Boreas rides in wrathful mood
  O'er all thy bleak domain;
He fiercely binds thy far-famed stream,
  He madly seals it fast,
And sweeps athwart thy dark ravines
  In many a roaring blast.

An hundred years great change hath brought
  To thy primeval state,
And in thy future's hidden years
  Still greater wonders wait;
Oh, glorious gate-way for the world,
  So kind to coming life,
Bring not the woes of Glencoe's vale,
  Nor old Thermopylae's strife.

Long ere Magellan built for fame
  By sailing round the earth,
In years unknown to history's page—
  Before Columbia's birth,
The tribal children here did dwell
  In freedom's happy dream,
And sought their food among the glens,
  And from thy fruitful stream.

But greater works thou wast to see
  Along thy rocky feet,
A graceful son thy river gave,
  The traveler's wants to meet;
And on its gentle bosom bore,
  In craft of wise design,
The treasures of the field and mill,
  And riches of the mine.

Anon the packet sped along
  In haughty, boastful pride,
Her precious load of joyous life
  Rode soft as zephyr's glide.

And swiftly by the wond'ring hills
　She carried man and wealth,
To distant fields they journeyed all
　For fortune or for health.

Yes, mark the wonder still to rise
　To men's progressive will,
The iron way traversed thy length,
　Men's wishes to fulfill;
And where thy quiet years have slept,
　The thund'ring train now flies,
And millions of the stirring race
　Have swept beneath thy skies.

Yes, every land that shares the sun
　Contributes to thy throne,
That day and night between thy slopes
　Is swiftly borne along;
And treasure, too, from every clime
　Comes slumbering in the wake,
And both are grateful for the way
　Thy kindly openings make.

And stretching all thy dreary length
　The iron nerves are hung,
That gather thoughts from all the world
　And speak with lightning's tongue;
What greater works hath man to boast
　Than these immortal peers
The telegraph, the telephone,
　That bless the rolling years.

And here—a century old to-day—
　Drake's Ferry lives in name;
How bright the story of its years,
　How far its patrons came!
What bustling life, what moving wealth,
　Confided in the skill
Of one tradition praises well
　And loves his memory still!

And last, let memory's deep impress
　Record the deeds of yore,
Of him who sleeps in peaceful rest
　On Juniata's shore;
Friend to friend, a foe to foe,
　To stand he was not slack,
And thou dost wear this hero's name—
　The name of Captain Jack.

1882
　　　　　　　　　　　　　　　　　　　W. W. FULLER.